Daughters of the Ark

Daughters of the Ark

by ANNA MORGAN

Second
Story
Press

Library and Archives Canada Cataloguing in Publication

Morgan, Anna, 1957-
Daughters of the ark / by Anna Morgan.

ISBN 1-896764-92-4

1. Jews--Ethiopia--Juvenile fiction. 2. Ethiopians-
Jerusalem--Juvenile fiction. I. Title.

PS8626.O743D39 2005   jC813'.6   C2005-900491-6

Edited by Sarah Silberstein Swartz
Copyedited by Leah LeDrew
Cover design and illustration by Peter Ledwon and Marilyn Mets
Text designed by P. Rutter

Printed and bound in Canada

*Second Story Press gratefully acknowledges the support
of the Ontario Arts Council and the Canada Council for
the Arts for our publishing program. We acknowledge the financial
support of the Government of Canada through the Book
Publishing Industry Development Program, and the Government
of Ontario through the Ontario Media Development Corporation's
Ontario Book Initiative.*

Canada Council   Conseil des Arts
for the Arts   du Canada

Published by
Second Story Press
20 Maud Street, Suite 401
Toronto, Ontario, Canada
M5V 2M5

www.secondstorypress.ca

In memory of Milton Turkienicz

Table of Contents

PART TWO – The Horn of Africa
Ethiopia, July 1984

PART THREE – The Long Journey
En Route to Jerusalem, August to November 1984

* * *

$\mathcal{P}$reface

O N JULY 13TH, 1985, Live Aid, a European super concert, came together to focus attention on the need for famine relief in Ethiopia. Musicians, including Phil Collins, Paul McCartney, and David Bowie, raised millions of dollars to help those that were affected by the crisis. More importantly, both the concert and the music's popularity raised awareness of one of the world's worst human catastrophes. It was hard not to be touched by the starvation that was spreading through Ethiopia.

During that time, the world wasn't paying much attention to a small number of Ethiopians known as the Beyta Israel, who lived in the northern parts of the country. These Ethiopian Jews were quietly leaving their villages and beginning to make their way to Sudan along with the many other Ethiopians who were looking for help. But for the Beyta Israel, it was more than the famine that prompted them to leave Ethiopia. After thousands of years in the Ethiopian mountains, the Beyta Israel hoped to return to their ancestral home.

1

Living in isolation for centuries, these Ethiopian Jews did not know of any other Jews in the world. They believed that the Jews outside of Ethiopia had been killed, scattered or exiled to Babylonia during raids on Jerusalem over 2,500 years ago. Over time, their elders had taught them that the responsibility to preserve the books of the ancient priests had been handed down to them from biblical time. As the only known Jewish community left in the world, they felt that it was up to them to make sure that the rituals and traditions of their ancestors would never disappear. When these Ethiopian Jews began to hear of a contemporary Jerusalem where other Jews lived together in their own country, they became interested in going to this county, Israel, and beginning new lives among their own people.

As a reporter, I began to interview some of these Ethiopian Jews. I became fascinated by their history and the stories they told me about the *Kebra Negast*, a legend about Prince Menelik, the son of King Solomon and the Queen of Sheba, who left Jerusalem with several Temple priests and their families. According to this epic tale, they had the Ark of the Covenant with them when they traveled to Ethiopia 3,000 years ago. I based the first part of my book on the Menelik legend.

In 2002, I met Shula Mola, the director of the Israel Association of Ethiopian Jewry, and have since that time spent many hours listening to her talk about the pilgrimages from northern Ethiopia to Sudan. She described how 12,000 Ethiopian Jews left their homes in 1984 because they had heard that a way to Israel was waiting for them in Sudan. Their journey was not an easy one; the walk through the deserts of Sudan was treacherous. While 8,000 people finally made it to Israel, more than 4,000 lost their lives on the way due to starvation and illness. I based the third part of my book on Shula's actual journey.

Two years later, I spent the summer in Ethiopia visiting the highlands and villages where Ethiopian Jews had lived. I interviewed men and women who remembered the days before the first pilgrimages began. *Daughters of the Ark* finally emerged as a fictionalized version of the legendary story and the historical one, with a description of life in Ethiopia in the 1980s tying them together.

Anna Morgan
February 2005

* * *

𝒫rologue
Ethiopia, 1979

EVER SINCE DEBRITU WAS A LITTLE GIRL, she knew about the legend of the emerald. "If you have the emerald, it will protect you," her mother used to tell her.

"Where did it come from?" Debritu asked her mother when she was nine years old.

"It came from Jerusalem, thousands of years ago," her mother answered, as they walked balancing their baskets of dirty clothes on their heads. They were on their way down to the banks of Angereve, one of the many rivers and creeks that ran into Lake Tana. On the dirt path, mother and daughter joined the other women from the nearby villages who were also walking to the river to do their washing.

"A young girl brought it with her all the way to Ethiopia," her mother continued, as she split a bar of soap into two for them to share. "But the girl vowed that the emerald would be returned to the Temple in Jerusalem one day. When she passed the jewel down to her daughter, she made her promise to return it as well."

"And then it was passed on from one generation to

5

the next," she added, as they scrubbed their clothes in the flowing water.

"Each family that gets the emerald is blessed and no harm will come to them, as long as they promise that one day the emerald will be returned to its home in Jerusalem," Debritu's mother explained.

"I bet it doesn't really exist," Debritu replied, skeptically, as the women lay their clothes out to dry on the grass by the river.

And yet, Debritu often wondered, what if the story of the emerald were true?

* * *

Part One

Leaving Home

Jerusalem in the Kingdom of Israel, 939 B.C.E.

Chapter One
ALEESHA

"OH, IT'S SO UNFAIR," ALEESHA GRUMBLED as she sat by her bedroom window. She folded her arms on top of the stone ledge and looked down at the celebrations. It was the first day of a new month and it seemed as if the whole city was out dancing and singing.

"They're all probably wondering why I'm not with them," Aleesha said to her mother, who was sitting at the east side of the window. The late afternoon sun cast bold streaks of light across the older woman's tired face.

"Please, Aleesha, stop complaining. You know there is a lot to do before we leave Jerusalem," she said to her daughter. "Besides, you don't have to worry about what your friends are saying. I'm sure they'll just think you're sick. By the time morning comes, we'll be ready to go."

"You don't understand, Ima," Aleesha said, addressing her mother. "It's not that I care what they say or think. It's just that I want to be out there, celebrating with them."

For most of the city of Jerusalem, today was a holiday — the first day of the month and almost everyone Aleesha knew was outside celebrating the Festival of the New Moon. She had just seen her cousin, Ruth, laughing and singing as she danced with the rest of their friends through the narrow alley that snaked its way just underneath Aleesha's balcony. Aleesha watched as the rays of the afternoon sun brightened the wreaths of lilies and garlands of palm that the dancers had woven into their hair, and she listened to the jangle of their necklaces and bracelets as they passed. The girls wore colored holiday tunics in shades of red and blue, along with their best belts with gold coins that dangled down the front.

Eventually, the festivities would end when everyone returned to their homes for a family meal. The sweet smell of lamb and cinnamon cooking in open-flamed fires was already beginning to fill the streets. Aleesha knew that by nightfall the gourds of wine prepared by the people of Jerusalem for special occasions would be emptied.

Jerusalem, the city in which Aleesha lived, had been built by King David only 50 years earlier to be the capital of the kingdom of Israel. Just before David died, he appointed his son Solomon to be the new monarch and instructed him to finish the construction of the city and its many buildings. King Solomon, who was known as a wise and just man, ruled over the 12 tribes of Israel and a kingdom which extended from the Galilean Hills on its northern border with Lebanon, to the Red Sea in the south where the king had established trade with Arabia, Egypt, and Ethiopia.

In Jerusalem, Solomon continued the work of his father building a magnificent Temple for the Israelites. Aleesha knew that although people came from all over the country to see the Temple, only certain people were actually allowed inside. Because Aleesha's father was one of the priests who worked in the Temple, he went inside every day. Men in Aleesha's family were born into their positions, a right that was passed from father to son. From a very early age, Aleesha's relatives studied the rules that would later become their responsibility to fulfill.

Within the Temple, it was the priests who took care of the daily rituals. Some of them lit the candelabras and incense. Others sounded the ram horns and golden trumpets that marked the opening and closing of the Temple gates. It was also part of their responsibilities to travel throughout the kingdom to teach the rest of the Israelites the laws that were set out on the tablets held inside the Ark of the Covenant, hidden at the center of the Temple.

The priests protected the Ark of the Covenant day and night because they held two sets of tablets on which were written the Ten Commandments. These commandments were the code of laws that the people of Israel followed. Their belief in these laws was the single most important sign of the unity of the Israelites after they were freed from slavery in Egypt and wandered in the desert for 40 years. Later, when the Israelites became known as the Jewish people, their belief in the Ten Commandments remained just as strong.

For several minutes, Aleesha watched the last few girls as they played their lutes and harps, moving through the narrow passageways until they disappeared around the corner. She waited for the last notes to fade into the air before she turned back to her sewing. Aleesha thought back on all the times she had celebrated the new moon with her friends.

"It's a holiday for everyone but us," Aleesha said bitterly. While the celebrations continued outside, mother and daughter were spending their day doing house chores.

"We're leaving in the morning and there is still plenty left to do," Ima said impatiently.

"But Ruth is also leaving in the morning. Yet she's out celebrating today," Aleesha complained.

"Your father wants everything ready by tonight," Ima said sternly. "There is no way we'll be done, if we don't stay home to finish our work."

"I'm having a hard time concentrating. I can't get much done anyway," Aleesha said, sighing. Her hands sewed over the same stitch for the third time. Finally she gave up, let the coarse threads slip through her fingers, and put the dress down on her lap.

"It's important that we sew a few nice things for the future. Who knows what we'll find in our new faraway home?" said Ima as she finished sewing the last few stitches on a white robe for her son Noam.

"Why can't I say goodbye to all my friends?" Aleesha asked sadly.

"You know Abba doesn't want everyone to know exactly when we're leaving. He was very strict about that," Ima said sternly, trying to convince her daughter that her father's instructions must be taken very seriously.

"Abba is in the Temple. He won't even know," Aleesha said.

"Whether he knows or not doesn't matter. You have to listen to what he says," Ima answered.

"I know," Aleesha said. "It's just that sometimes my head tells me to do one thing and my heart tells me something else."

"You must listen to your head," Ima said to her daughter, sighing. Ima knew it was sometimes hard to separate the two.

Aleesha looked at her mother and decided to stop asking to go out. She was never sure how far she could push her mother. There were days that she felt Ima was upset because Aleesha was so different from the other girls. Other times, she felt her mother was proud because of her independence. After all, it was Ima who had arranged for a teacher to come to their home every morning to teach Aleesha to read and write. Yet, Aleesha remembered how upset Ima was when she had caught her daughter crouched by the doorway, eavesdropping outside her father's room while he studied with the boys.

"You know that girls are not allowed to study with boys," Ima had chastised her daughter.

"I wasn't studying with them," Aleesha answered. "I was just sitting outside listening to them. Their discussions about the ways of the Temple are so interesting . . . ."

Before Aleesha could finish her sentence, Ima cut her off. "In our family, it is the boys' responsibility to study the ways of the Temple and girls must learn to be good wives. There is no need for girls to learn the ways of the priests. You know that is forbidden."

Quietly, Aleesha picked up the dress and sewed the last few cross-stitches on the embroidered gown, then she rested her chin on her arms and looked out the window again to see if anyone was still outside. She barely noticed the cool evening winds blowing into the city from the Judean hills, or the solitary hummingbird that hovered just next to her folded arms.

On the street, a group of Phoenician carpenters walked by, silently, their hammers and chisels hanging casually at their sides. King Solomon had worked hard to establish trading links with other kingdoms. On his country's western border, which touched the Mediterranean Sea, the king's royal fleet had forged routes into Spain, Greece, and Cyprus. He bought gold from Siamun, the Egyptian pharoah to the south, and cedar from King Hiram, who ruled over the northern kingdoms of Tyre and Sidon. A highway and coastal roads were built by King Solomon to develop economic ties with neighbors. People from the bordering countries came to Jerusalem to finish building the Temple, the palaces and the many courts that Solomon had started constructing.

Aleesha had gotten used to the foreign workers that were constantly coming to Jerusalem. Sometimes she would stop outside one of the palaces to watch the Egyptian and Nubian stonemasons chisel their designs with incredible skill, while Syrian carpenters brought in long tree trunks of cedar and wooden planks of cypress from Lebanon. In the evenings, Moabite laborers guided their donkeys through the narrow streets of Jerusalem to empty their baskets of rubble outside the city walls. The streets were always filled with the sounds of many different languages.

Now, she looked down and counted the ribbons scattered on the narrow, copper-colored cobblestone road where her friends had been dancing. Dried figs, almond shells and fresh dates were strewn on the street everywhere. Along the walls that bordered the street on both sides, jasmine vines covered the stones and framed the neighbors' windows. In the distance, she could still hear the sounds of voices singing, as the celebrators made their way to the Temple Square.

* * *

Chapter Two
SOLOMON, SHEBA AND MENELIK

"WHERE ARE WE GOING TOMORROW?" Aleesha asked her mother. "And how far will we be traveling?"

"We'll walk for many months across the deserts and arrive in a country called Habash. The sailors who trade with King Solomon's ships sometimes call it Ethiopia," Ima explained.

"Why are we going?" Aleesha asked.

"Because King Solomon ordered his high priest, Zadok, your grandfather, to send the 12 eldest sons of the Temple priests with his son, Prince Menelik, on his journey home to his people," Ima said with a sigh.

"Can't Abba simply refuse? Why must he go?" Aleesha asked.

"Zadok knows that he must send his own eldest son or he couldn't ask his brothers to send their eldest sons with their families. As Zadok's eldest son, your father must obey his father."

"Aren't you afraid?" Aleesha asked. Everyone knew that bandits controlled the land outside the safety of the walled city. Anything could happen without the king's guards to protect them.

"No," answered Ima, trying to sound convincing. "We won't be alone. We'll travel in a caravan with your cousins and together we'll make a home in the new land."

"Why is King Solomon sending Prince Menelik back to Ethiopia? And why does the king want us to go with him?" Aleesha asked.

Aleesha watched her mother as she put down her work, lifted the shawl that had fallen to her shoulders and carefully covered her head. Whenever Ima covered her head, Aleesha knew that her mother was going to say something important. It was something Ima did whenever she considered one of her daughter's many questions worthy of a serious reply. Aleesha just never knew which question her mother would take seriously.

"Prince Menelik's story began about 20 years ago when Makeda, the Queen of Sheba came to visit Jerusalem," Ima said, as she looked out their window into the Judean hills that lay in the distance, just beyond the limestone walls of their city.

"The queen, whom everyone here called Sheba, lived in Axum, the capital of Ethiopia, where she ruled over her people. She was so wise that people came from everywhere to seek her advice. She was so charming that even lions walked tamely by her side," explained Ima.

"She sounds much like King Solomon," Aleesha said, leaning back against the stone wall. As she listened to her mother's story, Aleesha slipped off her sandals and put her feet down on the cool, mosaic floor.

"Yes," Ima said, sighing. "They were like a match made in heaven. I was just a little girl then. And every afternoon I would go visit King Solomon's court with my brothers and sisters, so we could hear the queen tell us wonderful stories about her long trip from her land to Jerusalem. She had arrived with a caravan of camels that covered the hills as far as you could see. With her, she brought a ship filled with wood from the almug tree, a special type of timber that Solomon needed for his palaces."

"It was as if she knew ahead of time exactly what Solomon would need!" Aleesha exclaimed.

Ima continued, "On special days, she would let us unpack her snakeskin boxes and out would come spices, ivory, gold and precious stones. For every item, Sheba had an interesting story to tell. The queen's wealth, like her wisdom, seemed endless. Everyone could see that King Solomon loved the Queen of Sheba and that the queen loved him in return."

"Then why did she leave Jerusalem?" Aleesha asked.

Ima answered, "I guess she had her own kingdom to rule. You know, if a ruler stays away for too long, there is always the danger that someone will take over the kingdom. When she left Jerusalem, King Solomon was very sad and gave her his ring as a keepsake."

"Did she ever return to Jerusalem?" Aleesha asked, listening closely to every word of her mother's story.

"No, she never did. But then, just as suddenly, about 20 years later, a caravan came from Ethiopia with the queen's son, Menelik, wearing his father's ring. She had sent him to study with King Solomon and with the Temple priests," Ima said.

Aleesha knew that for the past two years, Menelik had spent long hours in the Temple, learning to read and write in Hebrew and studying with Zadok and the other priests. When Menelik had decided that it was time to go home and help his mother rule her kingdom, King Solomon had issued a proclamation that the 12 eldest sons of the Temple high priests would accompany Menelik to Ethiopia. King Solomon wanted to make sure that the prince could continue his studies and always remember the ways of his father.

"You know that when it comes to the king's orders, we have no choice," Ima said. "Once King Solomon issues a proclamation, no one can change his mind."

"I don't want to go to Ethiopia and I know that Abba doesn't want to go either," Aleesha complained. "Aside from Prince Menelik, I'll bet no one wants to leave Jerusalem."

Before her mother could respond, a loud crash brought Aleesha and Ima to their feet. The two women ran down the narrow stone stairs, their feet thumping as they raced to the courtyard at the back of their house. They made it just in time to see a man in a brown tunic slip around the corner.

* * *

Chapter Three
INTRUDER

"THIS IS TERRIBLE," Ima gasped at what she saw. In the courtyard at the back of the house, all their straw baskets and animal hide trunks had been packed away neatly, ready to be loaded onto the donkeys for the morning's journey. Now the containers lay open with their contents scattered about. Clothes and pots were dumped all around and clay dishes lay shattered on the ground. Aleesha and her mother looked at the mess with horrified amazement.

"We need to tell Abba what has happened," Ima said.

"Who would do this?" Aleesha asked. "And what were they looking for?"

"Whoever did this must have thought we would all be out celebrating and they could rummage through our things," Ima speculated.

"He must have heard us running down the steps and run away," said Aleesha, examining the mess.

"I am going to get your father from the Temple," Ima said as she ran into the house to get her cloak.

In the meantime, Aleesha looked around. It didn't seem

as though much had been taken. But someone had clearly been looking for something. Whoever it was had time to search through half of their trunks before one of the baskets must have unexpectedly fallen.

He probably didn't find what he was looking for, Aleesha thought, until she noticed an empty space between two baskets, where a trunk had once stood. One trunk was missing.

Why? Aleesha wondered. *What was in that trunk?*

Suddenly, Aleesha saw Ruth, her cousin and friend, coming toward her.

"Ruth, what are you doing here?" Aleesha asked.

"I was worried about you. Why weren't you out celebrating today? I came by to make sure you were alright. What has happened here?" Ruth asked, when she noticed the mess. "Are these your baskets?"

Ruth's father, Aaron, and Aleesha's father, Baruch, were cousins. The two girls, who looked alike with their black hair and dark almond eyes, did almost everything together. For years, their mothers got together every day, sometimes to weave sheep's wool into cloth, other times to sew new robes for their husbands and children. At their sides were their two daughters, Aleesha and Ruth.

Ever since they were little children, Ruth never minded that Aleesha, who was almost a year older than Ruth, took charge of their games and outings. In the long, hot

23

days that marked the dry season, Aleesha was always quick to organize their afternoons with hide-and-seek games that included all the neighborhood children. The thin, cobblestoned alleyways twisted and turned into perfect hiding spots for Aleesha and her friends.

As they grew older, Aleesha would take Ruth to explore all the corners of their city. Every morning, Aleesha and Ruth wrapped themselves in their cloaks, balanced their straw baskets on their heads, and wandered down into the parts of the city where the tradespeople and merchants lived. The girls loved looking at the shiny, new clay pots that were made by the potters. They couldn't resist touching the glossy black-and-white bolts of wool, still rank with the smell of the flocks of sheep that roamed the hills outside of Jerusalem. They carefully wound their way through the mounds of cucumbers, piles of melons, baskets of leeks, hampers filled with onions, and the heaps of tangled knots of garlic that filled the market. Smells of strange foods and spices from different lands hovered everywhere.

In the market, Ruth and Aleesha loved to compare the Israelite farmers from the Galilee, who brought fresh fish and pomegranates, to the Judean merchants, who came from the southern deserts with their leather goods. Their clothes, accents and gestures were all so different. Yet, they shared one religion and came to Jerusalem, not only for the market, but to see the Temple. Ever since

Aleesha could remember, the Israelites were drawn to the Temple, and the mysteries that were hidden inside.

Aleesha loved talking to the people in the market. But for the past few weeks, Aleesha didn't have much time to talk, because she was too busy bargaining with the merchants as she bought supplies for their upcoming trip. And now most of Aleesha's new purchases were scattered about in the alleyway.

"I don't know who made this mess," Aleesha said. "But, I want to find out."

"They were probably thieves, looking for gold and silver," said Ruth. "My mother says that thunderstorms and celebrations always bring out thieves."

"Maybe," Aleesha answered, slowly. "Except that the thief didn't take our silver platters or gold dishes." Aleesha pointed to the middle of the alleyway where the dishes were strewn on the ground. "I think he was looking for something else."

Just then, Aleesha's father, Baruch, came striding into the courtyard with Ima.

"Go home, Ruth, and you, Aleesha, please go inside the house," Baruch told the girls.

Aleesha hesitated as she watched Ruth turn the corner of the alleyway that led to her own house. Then Ima told her daughter, "Go inside until we come get you."

After Aleesha stomped up the stairs to her bedroom

and lit the oil lamp in the corner with a torch she had taken from the stone hallway, the restless 14-year-old girl went over to her bedroom window and looked out at the sun setting over the Judean hills. While the city was settling into the melancholy sleepiness that always followed a day of celebration, she could hear her parents in the courtyard going through the bags, whispering and repacking the baskets.

I'm so bored, Aleesha thought to herself as she looked through her window at the narrow road below. To her left, the road wound its way past the homes where the Temple priests lived with their families. It continued into town through the market, and eventually narrowed into the quarter where the peddlers, shoemakers and bakers lived. The web of streets ended at the city gate that was closed every night by the king's guards to prevent thieves from sneaking in. Aleesha sometimes stopped to watch the soldiers put down their bows and arrows, so they could pull the two heavy wooden doors shut before they slid the bolt across the middle. Then the king's brigade marched up to their posts across the top of the wall to watch out for potential invaders from the Judean desert to the east.

King Solomon's army was known for its chariots and horsemen, for their shields and their armor. But Aleesha was relieved that no invaders had actually attacked Jerusalem during her lifetime. She figured that it was just as well, since so many of the soldiers seemed to fall sound asleep, sitting at their posts.

From her window Aleesha looked to her right, where the road continued. She couldn't see past the end of her street, but she knew that the road eventually ended in the open square just outside the Temple. On one side of the Temple Square, there was a village of tents where the foreign workers lived while they worked on King Solomon's palaces. The courtyard on the other side of the square stood empty. Only the Temple priests dared to climb up the many stairs and through the Temple door to perform their daily rituals.

As the sun settled lower into the hills, Aleesha knew that it would soon be time to get ready for bed. This might be the last night she would sleep in her own room. The young girl began to make her bed, as she did every night, by spreading pillows over the bench. Then she continued her routine and checked to see if there was enough water left in the clay jugs to wash her feet before she got into bed.

Suddenly, Aleesha was fed up with her routines. She was annoyed at having spent the entire day in the house. It was so unfair that her brother could roam about freely. The thought of Noam out celebrating while she stayed inside all day upset her. On top of all that, someone had stolen their trunk and she wanted to find out why.

Aleesha decided to sneak out and take one last stroll through the streets of Jerusalem. *If anyone sees me, I'll say that Noam hadn't come home and I was worried and wanted to make sure he was alright,* Aleesha thought to herself. She quickly braided her hair, tied the long, black braid around her head, put on her sandals, pulled the cloak off her bed and wrapped it over her head and shoulders.

Outside, the rays of the setting sun had transformed the limestone walls into a pinky haze. It wouldn't be long before the sun settled behind the hills and the narrow alleyways fell into total darkness. Aleesha decided to run down to the Temple Square to see if anyone was still lingering from the day's festivities. If she hurried, she could make it down to the square and back before anyone noticed that she had disappeared.

* * *

Chapter Four
THE TEMPLE

ALEESHA GRABBED THE TORCH from the hallway and slipped out through the front door. Just a few doors from Aleesha's home, on the way to the Temple, Aleesha caught sight of Ruth sweeping her stone doorstep. Ruth's dark braids had come apart and her hair fell loosely to her waist.

"Aleesha, I thought you were supposed to stay inside your house," Ruth said. She hated it when her friend didn't listen to their elders. "Where are you going now?"

"I want to find out who was rummaging through our things," Aleesha said. "And I have a feeling that the answer is inside the Temple."

"The Temple!" Ruth said, startled.

"I'm going to go inside," Aleesha said, suddenly deciding that, more than anything else, this is what she wanted to do.

"Have you lost your mind?" Ruth asked her friend. "You know you're not allowed inside the Temple."

"If our brothers are allowed, why can't I go inside?"

Aleesha asked. Ruth's brother Benyamin and Aleesha's brother Noam both worked in the Temple as apprentices with their fathers. "I want to go inside just once before I leave."

"Do you know how much trouble you will get into, if you're caught?" Ruth asked her friend.

"I know," Aleesha said. "But think about it. In just a few hours, our families will be leaving. Everyone will be busy preparing for the trip. No one will be inside the Temple at this hour. If I don't try now, I'll never get another chance to be inside."

"Why do you want to go inside?" Ruth asked.

"Come with me," Aleesha begged. "Please. It's important. I want to see what my brother sees. I want to know what he knows. Besides, the answer to the intruder lies inside the Temple, I'm sure of it."

"How will you get past the guards?" Ruth asked.

"You'll be the distraction," Aleesha said. "And you can stay outside and warn me in case anyone else comes in tonight."

"Are you crazy?" Ruth asked.

"Ruth, nothing has ever been more important to me," Aleesha said. "I will never forgive myself if I don't try to go into the Temple before we leave Jerusalem."

"Alright, I'll go with you," Ruth answered slowly. "But I'm not going in. I'll wait outside. And you have to promise me you won't go anywhere near the Ark of the Covenant."

Both girls knew the stories about the Ark of the Covenant. Everything her family believed in was inside that Ark. Two sets of stone tablets, one whole and one broken, were safely hidden in the wooden container. On those tablets, given to her people in the deserts of Sinai, were written the laws and customs that guided King Solomon and his priests. Her father called the tablets the Ten Commandments.

Everyone knew that no one was allowed to touch the Ark. Aleesha and Ruth had been taught that anyone who even tried to look at the Ark would immediately burst into flames.

"I don't believe the stories about people bursting into flames for just looking at the Ark," Aleesha whispered.

"What are you saying?" Ruth said.

"I don't know," Aleesha said. "I'm not sure I believe there is anything wrong with just trying to see the Ark."

"Please, promise me you won't," Ruth pleaded.

"Alright, I'll try," Aleesha said.

"Okay, I'll help you," Ruth said, slowly. She knew how stubborn Aleesha was. It would be impossible to persuade her friend to change her mind. "Wait right here while I get my cloak."

Ruth went inside the small courtyard outside her

family's house to put her broom away and fetch her cloak. She didn't want anyone to hear her leave, so she tiptoed slowly back towards the front door. It took her a few minutes to find her cloak. Then she stopped in the courtyard to straighten up a basket of dates that had fallen on the ground. Reluctantly, Ruth closed the gate that separated her house from the street and checked to make sure it was shut tight.

By the time Ruth came out to join her friend, Aleesha was gone. And the torch Aleesha had been holding was on the ground, its flame extinguished.

* * *

Chapter Five
INSIDE THE TEMPLE

WHILE ALEESHA WAITED FOR RUTH, she heard the sound of a cough close by. She turned in the direction of the noise and spotted the man in the brown tunic who had run out of their courtyard just a few hours earlier. Aleesha was sure it was the intruder who had been rummaging through their things. She quickly put out the flame on her torch, dropped it and followed the man.

Making sure to stay well behind, she followed him through the empty streets until the road ended at the Temple Square. The square was now quiet and empty, after a full day of celebrations. All around the Temple, the construction workers had set down their tools on the marble-tiled square for the night. Aleesha watched as the man in the brown tunic slipped into the Temple, closing the curtained door behind him.

Each of the many stones of its walls was as tall as a camel and as wide as an elephant. It was easy to see why everyone said that the Temple stood like a mountain in the heart of the city. Aleesha thought about the time of day when the sun cast the Temple's huge shadow onto the square, just before the morning work began. But right now, quiet surrounded Aleesha, except for the soft whispers of a desert wind.

All of a sudden, Aleesha jumped. Ruth had come up to her from behind.

"Where did you go?" Ruth asked. "I thought you were going to wait for me."

"I saw the man in the brown tunic. He was the man who rummaged through our things. I followed him here," Aleesha whispered pointing to King Solomon's Temple. "And he went inside."

"Where are the Temple guards?" asked Ruth, puzzled.

Usually guards stood at the two pillars just outside the entrance to the Temple, not allowing anyone but the priests to enter. Tonight, there was no one there. From where they stood, the girls could see the two huge pillars of gold that stood in front of the Temple door, gleaming in the moonlight. In the middle of the square, a huge torch burned inside a copper bowl filled with olive oil. The light from the bowl, which rested on four wheels, was reflected in the gold pillars on both sides of the entrance. It shimmered and glistened like the sun's rays.

Slowly the girls crept closer to the Temple door. With the help of the torchlight, they could see the folds in the red velvet curtain that covered the door. They could feel the stillness of the desert night around them. Overhead, a few bats flew by, their wings visible in the cloudless, star-lit sky. In the distance, the jackals barked their hungry calls.

"Are you sure you want to do this?" Ruth asked her friend, hesitating. They had never been this close to the Temple before.

"I'm sure," Aleesha said, without looking at Ruth. "You wait behind that pillar," she said pointing to the golden column on the right. "If anyone comes by, whistle twice like a night bird. I'll be out before you know it."

Before Ruth could ask her friend how she would hear her whistles from inside the Temple, Aleesha had pushed the heavy red curtain aside and slipped inside.

It was so dark inside the Temple that Aleesha almost tripped over the two guards, fast asleep at the sides of the entrance. Plates of half-eaten food were on the floor next to them. *They were probably drugged,* Aleesha thought to herself. *Who could have drugged them?* she wondered.

As Aleesha turned towards the interior of the Temple, she couldn't believe how dark and quiet it was inside. The air was cool and Aleesha pulled her cloak tightly around her shoulders. If anyone walked by, the girl was sure they would hear the sound of her heart pounding right through her chest. She waited a minute to let her eyes get used to the darkness. Then she began slowly tiptoeing along, touching the gold-plated walls to keep her balance.

As she walked towards the center of the Temple, she noticed a strange smell of incense that kept getting stronger. Suddenly, she heard the sound of men talking and the thudding of their footsteps in the distance. She stopped and waited. Eventually, their voices disappeared.

Nervous about being caught, Aleesha considered leaving. But now, it would take her a few minutes to find her way back. Perhaps it was her brother she heard talking. If she moved quietly, maybe she could finally see what her brother did in the Temple. As she turned a corner, she found herself in front of two golden doors that stood higher than the tallest cedar she had ever seen. Aleesha pulled one door as hard as she could, but she could only get it to budge just wide enough for her to slip through. On the other side of the door was the most glorious room she had seen in her life.

This must be the sanctuary, Aleesha thought as she stood in a room bigger than anything she ever imagined. Ten golden, shining candelabras holding little cups filled with oil and burning wicks spread their light on one side of the room, and ten golden tables filled with the traditional loaves of bread covered the other. The ten candelabras and ten trays were a reminder of the Ten Commandments contained in the Ark of the Covenant.

For years, she had heard her father describe to her mother how he climbed three wooden steps to clean the oil out of the tall candelabras on the southern wall of the sanctuary. Breathlessly, Aleesha slid her fingers across the bottom of the candelabras. Then she slowly made her way towards the other side of the room where the ten tables for the loaves of bread stood. Each table had room for 12 loaves, with six shelves on each side.

One for each tribe of Israel, Aleesha remembered her father saying. Each tribe was descended from one of the 12 sons of Jacob – whose name later became known as Israel. Aleesha had heard her father teach her brothers about Jacob, who was descended from Isaac, the son of Abraham and Sarah.

In the middle of the room Aleesha could see the golden altar. She could smell the coals and incense burning on the altar and she watched the smoke rise into a spiraling swirl to the ceiling. For a minute, Aleesha let the smells surround her, and then she walked towards the wall in front of her, where a beautiful red curtain rose to the ceiling.

The curtain had five golden lions embroidered along one turquoise strip near its bottom and three golden eagles embroidered across another turquoise strip near its top. Two golden angels were carefully sewn in the middle.

I must be in the very heart of the Temple, Aleesha thought. This meant that the Ark of the Covenant was behind the curtain.

All of a sudden, Aleesha heard the sound of doors

closing and men's hushed voices talking as they came closer. Quickly, she snuck under one of the tables holding the sacrificial loaves of bread. Once she was safely underneath, she pulled down the curtain that covered the legs of the table.

"The Ark will be taken tomorrow, right after the priests finish their morning rituals," she heard a man say in a low voice.

"It is important that no one finds out about the plan," another man answered gruffly.

"What about King Solomon?" the first man asked. "Won't he send the army to bring it back?"

The men's footsteps passed and Aleesha could hear no more of their conversation. She slowly opened the curtain and pulled herself out of her hiding place. She could hardly believe what she had just heard. It seemed to be a plot to steal the Ark. She wanted to run home to her father to tell him everything. She wondered if he would even believe her. How would she convince him that the Ark was in danger?

Something inside Aleesha pulled her towards the red velvet curtain at the end of the room. *I'm so close to the Ark, the very heart of the Temple,* she thought. *How would it hurt anyone if I just took one quick look at the Ark? Maybe I'll be able to figure out some way of saving it, if I just look inside.*

Aleesha pulled open the curtains with all her might. She gasped when she saw the most beautiful box in the world. The Ark was made out of acacia wood and it was covered with a layer of pure gold. On each side were two golden rings and on top was a golden lid with two cherubs facing each other, their wings spread upwards. Resting on the Ark was a breastplate covered with gems.

Aleesha wasn't sure how long she stood there staring at the Ark. She felt as though she were in a dream. Then, suddenly, she thought of a way to convince her father about the plot she had overheard. Aleesha reached out and unfastened a beautiful shimmering emerald from the breastplate and slid it into her pocket.

When I show him this emerald, my father will have to believe that I was here, she reasoned.

In the distance, a door slammed shut, startling Aleesha out of her trance. Quickly, she turned to look around. No one was visible.

Aleesha had a strange sensation that someone had been watching her, but she couldn't see anyone in the sanctuary. Quickly, she headed towards the door and ran out of the Temple.

* * *

Chapter Six
A STRANGER

ALEESHA DIDN'T LOOK BACK AS SHE RACED through the dark Temple hallways, back to the front door and out into the starlit square. She found Ruth waiting for her behind one of the golden pillars and the two girls walked home while Aleesha told her cousin everything that had happened to her. The only thing she didn't tell Ruth was the part about the emerald. Aleesha decided that she would wait until after she told her father about the plot, before she told anyone else about the emerald.

"Remember your promise," Aleesha said, as the girls parted. "Not a word to anyone."

When Aleesha slipped quietly back into the house, her heart was still beating wildly. She climbed the narrow steps to her room and lit the lamp on the table next to her bench. She sat quietly for a few minutes, thinking about what had happened.

Aleesha would have to wait until morning, before telling her father what she had heard. When she walked by her parents' bedroom, her father wasn't in it. He probably had some last-minute things to arrange and wouldn't be back until morning. She put her hand inside her pocket and closed her fingers gently around the emerald. Inside her pocket, the emerald didn't feel like a jewel at all. Strangely, it felt soft and warm. Slowly, she took the emerald out of her pocket and relaxed her fingers, until the green jewel lay glimmering on the palm of her flat hand. Aleesha closed her hand around the emerald and felt its glow rise up her arms and fill her entire body. There was something very comforting about the energy that flowed from her hand through her arms and legs. It filled her with a sense of wonder. For safekeeping, Aleesha decided to sew the emerald into a fold on the inside of her cloak.

Only when the emerald was safely hidden inside her cloak did she allow herself to think about what she had done. *What will I do when they notice the missing jewel? How will I ever explain? What could have possessed me to even look at the Ark? And what about the plot to steal the Ark?* Aleesha knew that she had to tell her father about the men who were scheming to steal the Ark. But how would she explain what she had been doing inside the Temple?

As she tossed back and forth, Aleesha decided that the only thing she could do was put the jewel back into the breastplate before they left Jerusalem. *In the morning, I'll go into the Temple one more time and put the emerald back,* she promised herself. *Then I'll tell Abba right away about what I overheard. I know he'll believe me. He'll see I'm right when he catches the thieves.* After she had made her decision, she felt more calm and fell asleep.

Before long, it was morning, and Aleesha was awakened by roosters crowing in the distance. From her bed, she listened to the familiar sounds of the city stirring, as workers began to get ready for the day. Just outside her window, a donkey groaned as its owner called out for the city's garbage. Clay pots clanked as the farmers arranged their array of fresh milk and eggs to sell in the market. Flocks of sheep bleated as they were being herded outside the city walls. The sun was just beginning to rise when Aleesha stretched and got up to wash and dress. It was still very early in the morning.

Yawning, Aleesha picked up one of the empty water jugs to fill at the city well, one last time. From the well, it would be easy to slip into the Temple while everyone was getting ready for their trip. Aleesha put on her cloak and lifted the water jug onto her shoulder. She closed the door and began her walk down the path towards the city well.

In just a few hours, Aleesha and her uncles, aunts and cousins would gather at the city gates, where their caravan would be waiting for them. Aleesha felt a nervous grumble in her stomach every time she thought about the trip. So much had happened in just one day, and there were so many questions left unanswered. Who were the men inside the Temple who planned to steal the Ark? Who was the intruder in her own home?

As Aleesha got closer to the well, she noticed two people huddled together by the circular stone fence that prevented the goats and sheep from straying too close to the well. Even though this was one of the few spots where everyone gathered to pull up the fresh spring water from underneath their city streets, it was usually abandoned this early in the morning.

Strange, she thought, as she approached. *Meetings don't usually take place by the well at this time in the morning.* At a safe distance, she stopped and hid behind an old tamarind tree. From where she was standing, Aleesha could see that the person facing her was a man, about her brother's age, with fair hair and blue eyes. He was clearly a stranger to the city. His tunic was made from expensive white cottons and had gold threads running through it. A belt was tied around his waist and held his water bottle and a pouch. The brown stripes running down each side of his robe were the patterns from the tribe of Naphtali, the Israelites who lived in the Galilee, in the northern part of the country.

The city gate is probably still closed. I wonder how he got in so early in the morning, Aleesha thought.

As she listened cautiously, she heard the older man say, "Welcome to Jerusalem." As soon as she heard his voice, Aleesha realized that it was her father.

"I have received a note from my brother in the north saying it is important that I meet with you," Baruch said. "Who are you and where are you from?"

"I am Joseph from the tribe of Naphtali," the stranger said, as he sat on the edge of the stone fence around the well.

The kingdom of Israel was divided into 12 provinces, one province for each tribe. The tribes of Naphtali, Dan, Asher, Zebulun, and Issachar inhabited the northern part of the kingdom. Those of Simeon, Judah, Benyamin and Ephraim lived in the south. The tribes of Manasseh, Gad and Reuben lived in the east, on the other side of the Jordan River among the Moabites and Ammonites.

King Solomon, himself, was a descendent of the tribe of Judah, whose people lived in Jerusalem, as well as in the southern part of the kingdom. Solomon sometimes gave special preference to his own tribe. They worked for him in Jerusalem so he exempted them from taxes and from work in the copper mines. Other tribes, especially those in the north, began to resent the king for this special treatment.

One of King Solomon's supervisors, Jeroboam, sensed the unrest amongst the tribes and tried to organize a revolt against the king. Although he gained some support, most of the kingdom remained loyal to King Solomon. But trouble was brewing in the north.

"Tell me, Joseph," Baruch said. "My brother writes that the people of Naphtali are unhappy with the king. Is that true?"

"A rebel in the north has convinced the people that they should stop paying their taxes. He tells them that it is too much for them to pay," Joseph said.

"But King Solomon needs money to pay for the workers who are building his palaces and maintaining the Temple, for the court judges and for the soldiers in his army who protect us from invaders. Have the leaders not explained this?" Baruch asked.

"The people in the north don't understand why they need palaces, the Temple or a court so far from their homes. They have been persuaded by the rebels that they would be better off if they were protected by their own army, and ruled by their own leaders," Joseph said.

"And you? Do you believe that the north should separate and form its own kingdom?" Baruch asked.

"No," Joseph answered. "My father was a sailor who worked in King Solomon's fleets. He told me how well people talk of King Solomon and his wisdom all around the world. I believe we are much stronger and can achieve great things, if we listen to King Solomon and remain united."

"I see," Baruch said quietly.

"But not everyone agrees. Rebels are telling the northerners that the only solution is to revolt against the king, steal the Ark of the Covenant and separate from the king-dom," Joseph continued.

"What else do you hear?" Baruch asked.

"A man named Jeroboam is gathering an army against the king. He once worked for King Solomon and knows the country well," Joseph said.

"I met him," Baruch said. "He served the king for many years. Is he popular in the north?"

"Yes. The people like him and it won't be long before his army is strong," Joseph said.

"I will warn the king. In the meantime, send this to the priests in the north as quickly as you can. They will understand what to do with it," Baruch said, and then he handed a parcel to Joseph.

"What is it?" asked Joseph.

"It is a map of a certain city in Egypt," Baruch said. "The priests will find something very precious waiting for them there."

"As you wish. I will make sure that the map finds its way to your brothers in the north," Joseph said, bowing slightly.

"Good luck," Baruch said and walked back in the direction of the Temple, while Joseph walked towards the well.

Aleesha waited until her father had disappeared, before she approached the well. Joseph filled his pouch with water, as she leaned over to fill her water pot.

"What brings you to Jerusalem?" Aleesha asked him in a friendly, innocent manner.

"I am a visitor to your city," Joseph answered.

"Are you here for long?" Aleesha continued.

"Do girls in Jerusalem always ask strangers so many questions?" Joseph asked, laughing.

"It is just very unusual to see a stranger at the well so early in the morning. I was just wondering why you are here," Aleesha said.

"Well, I suggest that young girls leave strangers to come and go as they please," Joseph said, as he turned away from the well, tucking the parcel under his arm. He soon disappeared into the gray alleys of the city.

* * *

Chapter Seven
THE ARGUMENT

IT WAS STILL QUIET IN THE CITY and Aleesha finished filling her pot, put it on her head and turned to walk towards the Temple, wondering how she would slip inside to return the emerald. Her thoughts were interrupted by the sound of loud voices in one of the alleys nearby. Aleesha could hear the voices of men arguing, so she hid behind a corner, careful not to get too close.

"I found the trunk," she heard one man say. "But someone had been there before me. When I got the trunk home and looked inside, it was empty. I even checked in the Temple last night. But there was no sign of the map anywhere."

That must be the man in the brown tunic, Aleesha thought.

"How could that be? Only two men knew the map was inside that trunk. One was Baruch and the other one was you," said another voice.

"Are you accusing me of double crossing Jeroboam?" the man in the brown tunic asked.

"Jeroboam told me that some of his men saw you with King Solomon just the other day," the other voice said with a sinister edge.

"I did not tell King Solomon a thing," the man in the brown tunic responded.

"The map is very valuable. Maybe you sold it to someone else," the other man said.

"Please believe me, I did not betray Jeroboam," said the man in the brown tunic.

Aleesha heard what sounded like a scuffle and saw one man running off. He was covered from head to toe in a dark black cloak. She waited quietly behind the corner of the alley, until it grew quiet. Then she slowly crept closer. When Aleesha reached the spot from which the sounds had come, there seemed to be no one around.

She was just about to turn away, when she saw a man's arm stretched out lifelessly from the heaps of garbage piled in the corner of the alley. As she got closer, she could see a dagger lying nearby, drenched in blood. "Oh no!" she exclaimed.

The man in the brown tunic was dead.

* * *

Chapter Eight
THE CARAVAN LEAVES

"YOU ARE FREE TO GO," the court of elders finally announced to Aleesha, after she had told them everything she had heard and seen in the alley.

"While it would seem that the man in the brown tunic was from the north, no one seems to know who he was or what he was doing in the city of Jerusalem. There doesn't seem to be much point in continuing the investigation," the senior judge pronounced. In ancient Israel, community elders and scholars played the interchangeable role of police and judge. Without an eyewitness, it would be impossible for the elders to proceed with an accusation or a trial.

Aleesha ran home to gather the last few things she had left scattered around her room.

She wrapped her cloak around her tightly and grasped the emerald in her hand for a few seconds. The investigation meant that Aleesha couldn't get back into the Temple to return the jewel to the Ark. Nor did she have a chance to tell her father about the plot she had overheard.

Now her father and the rest of the group were anxiously waiting for her to begin the journey, which had already been postponed by several hours.

For the time being, Aleesha decided she would keep the gem with her, safely hidden in her cloak. Inside her room, Aleesha stood at her window and looked out at Jerusalem and the Judean hills surrounding the city.

"I will miss you," Aleesha whispered, and wiped her eyes with her sleeve. "And I will never forget my promise to return the emerald to you," she added, as she closed the door to her home for the last time, and ran through the narrow streets towards the gates of the city.

By the time Aleesha arrived, the group was already outside the walled city, mounted on their camels and horses, ready to set out. Prince Menelik was at the front, sitting on a tall, white horse. The priests and their sons followed him closely, some on horses and others on camel. The women and children rode behind. In the very center of the group, guards protected the camels and horses that were carrying the sacred books from the Temple that the priests were bringing with them. At the very back, donkeys and mules carried their personal belongings.

"I thought we might have to leave you behind," Ruth said as Aleesha found her camel and quickly settled into her place in the group next to Ruth.

They were beginning their journey just as the sun was

at its peak, in the center of the sky. Eventually, the evening breeze would find its way into the desert valley to cool them. But in the meantime, it was hot in the hills around Jerusalem. Aleesha soon took her cloak off and draped it over her camel. Most of the other women used their cloaks to sit on, but Aleesha rolled hers up carefully and tied it to the side of her camel with her water bag, where it would be safe.

From time to time, Aleesha touched the emerald hidden in the folds of her cloak. Strangely, the feel of its shape gave her some comfort as they traveled further and further into the hot desert. The sand glistened like specks of gold all around them, and wild eagles flew overhead in the cloudless sky.

"We may never see Jerusalem again," Ruth said, as the two cousins watched the walled city grow smaller in the distance. As they began to descend into the valley that would block their view of Jerusalem, the girls looked back as the last of the city's stones disappeared into the drifting sand.

"Don't look back," Aleesha said to her friend as she guided her camel towards the front of the group. Suddenly, Aleesha noticed that Joseph, the man she had seen at the well, was riding up front, near her father.

"Who is that man?" Aleesha asked Ruth, pointing to Joseph.

"Which one?" Ruth asked.

"The one who is barely older than us, yet he gets to ride up ahead with my father," Aleesha said curtly.

"He is a friend of the king," Ruth answered. "Your father introduced him to everyone before you arrived. He will be our guide to our new home."

* * *

Chapter Nine
IN THE JUDEAN HILLS

A S THE GROUP BEGAN THEIR EASTERN DESCENT through the Judean hills and into the valley, the only thing they could see was sand and desert scrub. To the north, Aleesha could make out the city of Jericho where the heat seemed to shimmer off the stones and rise in wavy lines towards the sky. Market noises from the bustling town traveled through the silent desert air. Aleesha thought she could hear the sound of tambourines and drums in the distance. As they kept riding further into the sandy hills, lonely cactus bushes and solitary date palms began to replace the towns and villages that dotted the hillsides just outside Jerusalem.

"What do you think we'll find in Ethiopia?" Aleesha asked.

"Maybe bazaars and houses just like at home," Ruth said. "You know, I think it will be quite nice to settle in a new place and make new friends . . . ." Ruth's voice faded as the sound of the evening wind picked up and Aleesha could barely hear a single word her friend said.

As night fell, the group drifted in the desert hills like a lone ship sailing ocean waters. The group had little to protect them from the biting wind and flailing sand. The desert air was cooling down quickly. Even when she put her cloak around her, Aleesha could not stop shivering.

It was time to stop for their first night in the desert. Aleesha and Ruth quickly set to work, helping to put up the tents. As she worked, it seemed to Aleesha that their caravan could easily be mistaken for a nomadic clan crossing the desert on their way to an oasis.

By the time their belongings were unloaded and the animal-skin tents were set up, the center of their camp stretched out like a small village. Aleesha watched while the camels were gathered on the outskirts of the camp, and the older boys were sent to watch over them. The sheep and cattle were tied up, with the younger boys and dogs at their sides. The women started unloading the pots for cooking, and the younger girls and servants were sent to watch over the babies.

Two goats were taken away to be slaughtered and cleaned. The women started the fires for cooking and the servants began washing the beans and vegetables. Ima took charge of one pot and Ruth's mother took charge of another. Before long, the smells of coriander and stewed meat began to fill the campsite.

While the women busied themselves with the dinner,

Aleesha and Ruth set out to explore. The girls walked around their temporary campsite, helping some of the others finish pitching their tents. When Aleesha got to her brother's tent, she stopped to see what he was doing. Inside, she could see that her brother was hunched over a book with a few of his friends. While Ruth walked ahead to talk to some of the other girls, Aleesha settled into a comfortable position next to the tent opening where she could hear the boys' discussion.

"The map was definitely in the stolen trunk," Noam announced.

"What does that mean?" Ruth's brother Benyamin asked.

"It means that someone knows exactly where we are going and what route we'll take," Noam replied.

"Then we must convince your father to change the route," Benyamin added. "Otherwise we will be followed and the Ark will be in danger."

The Ark? Here? Is my brother one of the thieves? Aleesha wondered as she hid behind the flaps of the tent.

"Agreed," Noam said. "But there is another problem. A stone is missing and no one knows who took it."

"Maybe the thief who took the trunk also took the emerald," said Benyamin.

"Clearly, someone is trying to steal the Ark. But why would they steal only an emerald?" Noam asked.

When Aleesha heard the boys moving about, she crawled away from their tent. Then she stood up and walked back towards the opening, pretending she hadn't been listening.

"Have you unpacked yet?" Aleesha asked her brother, as she entered the tent. His tent was covered in beautiful red carpets with cushions spread around the floor.

"It is not your concern," Noam said to his sister, gruffly.

"Why can't you ever be nice to me?" Aleesha asked her brother.

Noam stopped and for a second Aleesha thought her brother would tell her what was really on his mind.

"I suggest you keep yourself out of trouble," he said, this time more gently.

Insulted, Aleesha walked out of the tent. *Noam is only one year older than me,* thought Aleesha, *but he thinks he is so important. He acts as if he is already a priest and not just a student.*

Suddenly, Aleesha spotted Joseph again – the young man from the well and her father's trusted guide. He was running away from the caravan and into the hills. Aleesha quickly followed him, making her way around the tents and away from the families as they prepared for the coming night. She watched the young man climb the first hill. Aleesha tried to follow as Joseph reached the top of the first sand dune. "Joseph," Aleesha called as she reached the top of the hill.

But when she looked around, he was nowhere to be seen.

* * *

Chapter Ten
SANDSTORM

A S THE DAYS PASSED, Aleesha and Ruth learned to put up their cowhide tents more quickly and to unroll the sheepskin carpets that made their desert dwellings into homes. They became experts at taking down their tents and loading them onto their horses and camels, along with their pots and dishes. And they learned to ride their camels faster than anyone in their group.

The girls learned to rise before the hot sun made it impossible to work. They learned to wait until the fireball finally set into the dunes, before they began setting up their tents. Aleesha began to understand the importance of watching the water supply in her leather-skinned pouch carefully. She began to count the days between stops where water wells were available for wanderers.

For weeks, the group journeyed in the desert, sometimes walking, sometimes riding on their horses and camels, up and down the sandy hills and dunes. Finally they came to an oasis called Be'er Sheva.

"We will stop here for awhile before we decide which

route to take to Ethiopia," her father told the group. "We could cross Be'er Sheva to the west and continue on through Egypt. Or we could proceed further south, past King Solomon's copper mines at Timna and on to Aqaba, before going east through Arabia," Baruch explained.

"Why would we want to go through Egypt?" Noam asked.

"We have gold and silver to trade for food and water with the Egyptian people," Baruch reasoned.

"The route through Arabia is mainly desert," Noam said. "It might be hot and dry, but no one will bother us if we go that way. I think it makes more sense to travel through Arabia."

"If we go through Arabia, there will be a problem finding food and water," Baruch insisted.

"Who knows the difficulties we will find on our way through Egypt?" Noam responded. "Weren't our people enslaved in Egypt to satisfy the pharaoh? How can we forget this so quickly?"

"But King Solomon now has good relations with the pharaoh. It is foolish to try to make our way through Arabia. How will we find water? We have no sense of the place," Baruch answered sternly. "I will think about it. In the meantime, we will camp here." And so the caravan pitched their tents and began getting ready for a lengthy stay.

"Whatever way we go, we will be leaving Solomon's kingdom very soon," Ima told her daughter one morning, while they were boiling leaves to make tea.

"Has Abba decided which route we will take?" Aleesha asked, pouring the tea for her mother.

"Not yet," Ima said.

"What is Abba worried about?" Aleesha asked.

"He is concerned that we are being followed and that, in Arabia, it will be easy for thieves and bandits to attack us," Ima said.

"Why doesn't Noam want us to travel through Egypt?" Aleesha asked.

"Noam believes that whoever stole the map will try to ambush our group. He has heard that Jeroboam, the rebel from the north, is hiding along the route to Egypt," Ima said.

"So there is danger no matter which way we go," Aleesha said, sighing.

"Your father will figure out a way to keep us safe," Ima said, trying to sound confident.

"When do we leave?" Aleesha asked her mother.

"In the morning," Ima answered. "The decision will be made in the morning."

Aleesha wandered to the outskirts of the camp and looked out into the desert. The evening winds were beginning to blow and Aleesha pulled her cloak around herself to prevent it from blowing away. Without thinking, she touched the spot where she had sewn the emerald. As she reached the last tent, Aleesha could have sworn that she heard the sound of a shepherd's flute in the desert dunes.

Who could be out in the desert at this time of day? Aleesha wondered as she walked into the dunes towards the musical notes. She was so intent on following the sound of the music that she barely noticed that the wind was blowing harder and sand was nipping at her ankles. Soon, the sand began to twirl around her legs, and the ground underneath her feet began to shift and sink.

Suddenly, Aleesha realized that she was caught in a desert storm. She wrapped her cloak even tighter around her body and tried to look around as she pressed back in the direction of the campsite. But the wind had started to blow so wildly, she couldn't make out which way to go. For the first time in her life, Aleesha was really frightened. She had lost control.

As the wind tossed her about, she tried to keep walking. The sand underneath the soles of her feet felt like the strong pull of an ocean tide tugging her in one direction, while the wild wind swept her in the other. Strangely, she could still hear the sounds of the flute, until she dropped, exhausted, into the shifting sands.

When she woke up, Aleesha was in a dark cave and Joseph was sitting next to her. He held a water pouch to her lips and squeezed some drops into her mouth. Next to him was a flute.

"It was you," Aleesha said. "You were playing the flute. I knew I heard music."

"Yes, it was me," Joseph laughed. "But you weren't supposed to wander off into the desert."

"What are you doing here?" Aleesha asked, remembering the first time she had seen him by the side of the well in Jerusalem.

Joseph got up and walked towards the entrance of the cave. Aleesha followed him and looked out at the desert. The storm had passed and Aleesha could see the caravan in the valley below.

"Who are you and why are you hiding in the caves when you are supposed to be guiding my father?" Aleesha asked.

"I've been sent by King Solomon to protect your family," Joseph said.

"Protect?" said Aleesha, surprised.

"Why do you sound so shocked?" Joseph asked.

"Because I thought you took the map from my father and handed it over to the rebels." Aleesha finally confronted Joseph with her suspicions. "What I haven't been able to figure out is why," she announced.

Chapter Eleven
THE SECRET

"DID YOU BETRAY MY FATHER?" Aleesha asked Joseph. "No," Joseph answered, firmly.

"So, why do you leave the group and run into the hills?" Aleesha asked.

"Because King Solomon ordered me to watch over your caravan," Joseph said.

"Why?" Aleesha asked.

"King Solomon wanted to make sure that his son and the priests arrive safely in Ethiopia. And besides, you have the Ark of the Covenant with you," Joseph said with a smile, knowing that Aleesha would be startled by the news.

"We have it with us on the caravan? We took it from the Temple? Why?" Aleesha asked, hoping that she would finally find out the truth from Joseph.

"For months now, Jeroboam has been trying to steal the Ark from the Temple. He believes that if he manages to capture the Ark, people will recognize him as their true monarch. When King Solomon discovered the plot, he decided it would be wise if Menelik and your father's group took the Ark with them to Ethiopia for safekeeping. But spies betrayed the king and told his enemy that Solomon was planning to send the Ark with your caravan. So Jeroboam sent one of his men to steal the map that showed the route of your journey. He hopes to ambush your caravan on the way," Joseph said.

"Did Jeroboam send the man in the brown tunic to steal the map? Was that the man who was killed in the alley in Jerusalem?" Aleesha asked.

"Exactly," Joseph responded. "When he couldn't find the map, Jeroboam was convinced that the man in the brown tunic had betrayed him, so he sent in one of his henchmen to kill him.

"So, King Solomon secretly sent the Ark away with us," Aleesha said, finally understanding why the men in the Temple had been planning to take the Ark after the morning rituals.

"Yes, for the time being, King Solomon thought the Ark would be safer with you," explained Joseph.

"And will the Ark stay in Ethiopia with us?" asked Aleesha, puzzled.

"I don't know," Joseph said, mysteriously. "I guess that will be up to King Solomon. But in the meantime, we have another problem."

"What do you mean?" Aleesha asked.

"Look over there," Joseph said, pointing to the dunes directly across the desert plains.

"Those men have been watching your group very closely for some time," he said.

In the distance, Aleesha could see two small black tents pitched against the wall of a dark desert valley.

"How many are there?" Aleesha asked, looking over at the tents.

"So far, I've seen only five men," Joseph said. "But there may be more hiding in the hills. In the meantime, my job is to watch and make sure that the Ark is safe. I've sent word back to King Solomon that you are being followed and you might need help along the way." He added, "The only thing we haven't been able to figure out is who took the missing emerald. Now, you better get back to your family before they send out scouts looking for you," said Joseph, as he walked her down the hill. While they had been talking, the wind had completely disappeared and the sun started to set behind the newly formed sand dunes.

* * *

Chapter Twelve
A DECISION IS MADE

THE SMELL OF FLATBREAD AND LAMB STEW SIMMERING over the open flames filled the air. Even though Aleesha missed the taste of the sweet grapes, tart pomegranates and sour lemons that her mother used to liven up their meals at home, she knew that for the Sabbath tonight, they still had enough salt and dried garlic to spice up the cooking.

"It's getting late. Go get ready for the Sabbath," her mother called out to her.

By the time Aleesha brushed her hair and changed into her white Sabbath tunic, the women had already begun to gather under Ima's tent, with food to share and stories to tell. The men gathered together on the other side of the caravan. As the stars began to blanket the sky, the women danced and sang, voicing their hopes that the journey would soon end safely.

When Aleesha grew tired, she came inside the tent to get her dinner. "*Labreeyute,*" Ima said to her daughter, passing her a plate filled with bread and lamb stew.

"To your good health, too, Ima," said Aleesha, as she took the plate from her mother.

The women stayed up together until late into the night, knowing that the next day was the Sabbath, and that the caravan would rest until the day was over. Aleesha always hated for the Sabbath eve to end and she tried to make it last as long as possible. She stayed up with the women talking and laughing until the last of the night's darkness began to melt away with the sun's morning rays.

"We will be leaving the day after tomorrow," Ima said to her daughter before they finally lay down to sleep. "After tomorrow night's meal is finished, we will begin packing up."

"Which route are we taking?" Aleesha asked her mother, anxiously.

"Your father has not yet told us," Ima answered.

Aleesha barely slept a minute before she got up a few hours later to see if Ruth had heard anything about their upcoming journey. The past few days had been so busy that she hadn't spent much time talking with her friend. They had a lot of catching up to do.

"We're being watched," Aleesha told Ruth.

"What do you mean?" Ruth asked her friend, looking around her.

"Bandits and rebels are watching us from the hills," Aleesha said and then began to explain to her friend what she had seen with Joseph.

"Shouldn't we tell the elders?" Ruth asked, finally sitting down beside her friend.

"What good will it do?" Aleesha said. "Besides, I don't think they would believe me. Or worse yet, they'll confine me to my tent for leaving the caravan."

"I'm going to tell my father," Ruth said.

"No," Aleesha said. "Don't tell anyone. Joseph assured me that King Solomon has been alerted. If you tell anyone now it might get in the way of the king's plans. Promise me you won't."

"Alright," Ruth said, sighing. "But promise me you'll tell me everything that happens from now on."

After the girls finished talking, Aleesha walked around the campsite to see what information she could find from others. She stopped to chat with her uncles and aunts, as they began packing their belongings and tying up their parcels. Everyone knew that in the morning, the caravan would be leaving Be'er Sheva.

As she wandered to the middle of their desert village, Aleesha knew she was getting closer to the area of the campsite where she was not allowed to go. It was permissible only for the Temple priests and their students to walk into the white tents that were pitched in a circle in the middle of the group. The tents held the sacred books and ceremonial vessels. Aleesha suspected that the tents also held the Ark of the Covenant. As she walked by, Aleesha could see her brother and cousins, deep in discussion. Aleesha made her way past her brother's tent to the big white awning at the heart of their little village.

The awning had four velvet curtains that covered each side. A guard stood at its entrance.

How could I get inside? Aleesha wondered as she tripped over a small rock on the dusty path. She picked it up and threw it so that it landed with a thud a few tents away. When the guard went to investigate, Aleesha quickly ran to the entrance and peered inside.

Behind the curtain, in the middle of the tent, stood the Ark and breastplate she had seen in Jerusalem. And there, in the middle of the breastplate, was an empty spot where the emerald was missing.

I could return the emerald right now, Aleesha thought.

But, before she could act, she heard the sound of the guard grumbling as he walked back towards the tent. Quickly, she dropped the curtain and ran back to her mother's tent before the guard saw her.

"Help me pack up," Ima instructed when she saw her daughter. The women worked together, getting ready for the trip the following morning. They loaded the camels and mules with their woven blankets, straw baskets and clay pots filled with water.

"Go get some sleep, now," Ima told her daughter.

"You will need your rest for the journey tomorrow."

Aleesha was so exhausted from the evening's work that she soon fell sound asleep. When she got up in the morning, Aleesha wondered where the day would take them.

"The next stop we make will be in Egypt," Ima said. "We'll stay out of the villages until we get to the city of Elephantine. It will be possible to trade our wares for fresh fruits."

"You mean we won't be going through Arabia?" Aleesha asked.

"Your father has decided to take the route through Egypt," replied Ima. "Your brothers have found a guide who will direct us."

The tents were packed up. The camels and horses were loaded with the last few things and the group was back on its way before the start of the day. Before too long, the hot sun burned down on Aleesha's face, which she covered with her cloak to keep the sand from flying into her eyes. Every once in a while, she uncovered her eyes to look into the desert hills, checking for signs of bandits.

* * *

Chapter Thirteen
ELEPHANTINE

ALEESHA'S GROUP WANDERED FOR SEVERAL WEEKS. Sometimes, where there were no villages or towns, they clung close to the Nile River. At other times, they veered out into the Egyptian desert. They stayed out of the cities for fear of bandits. But by the time they neared the city of Elephantine, which was founded on a small island in the Nile River, they were down to the end of their supplies. In the morning, a group would go into town, by boat, to trade copper from Solomon's mines in exchange for fruits and vegetables.

"I want the men to go into town to learn what they can about the news of the day. The women will go trade and bargain for the food we will need for the next part of the journey," Baruch ordered.

"Please let me go with the women," Aleesha pleaded with her father.

"You must promise to stay out of trouble," Baruch warned her. "The town will be filled with strangers from different countries. If you go, you will be there to help your mother. You must stay with her and listen to everything she tells you." He paused for a moment.

"Understood?" Baruch asked, with a raised eyebrow.

"Absolutely," Aleesha answered, running over to give her father a hug. Baruch glanced at his shrewd daughter. He knew that she would be the only one of the women who would bargain hard for the best possible prices. But more importantly, she would be on the constant lookout for trouble. He had decided to send her into town for a reason.

As they boarded the boats that would take them to the island city of Elephantine, Aleesha thought about her father and how hard it must be for him. As the high priest's eldest son, the safety of the group was his responsibility. Aleesha remembered seeing her father when travelers came from all over King Solomon's kingdom to the Temple in Jerusalem. Aleesha would stand with the crowds at the bottom of the Temple steps, while they watched Baruch and the other Temple priests in their white robes and turbans, performing the holiday rituals.

"We are nearing the city of Elephantine," someone yelled out, interrupting Aleesha's thoughts. Soon they were able to disembark.

As they walked towards the center of town, they saw where the merchants were selling their camels, mules, donkeys, sheep and cattle. Further on, Aleesha could see piles of ivory tusks being sold.

Once they reached the town center, Aleesha forgot about everything else, as she busied herself with buying their supplies. Along each side of the gray road, men and women were selling clay pots, copper trays, ivory cups, colorful carpets, embroidered pillows, chickens and roosters, fruits and nuts of all kinds and vegetables she had never seen before. Robes, cloaks and leather pouches hung from the canopies built into the sides of the stone houses. Bolts of wool and flax were piled inside the stalls, alongside threads and yarns that were dyed every imaginable color.

While her brother sat down to drink tea with the other desert travelers, Aleesha and her mother stopped at the merchants' stands to look for the freshest pomegranates, the plumpest dates and the juiciest lemons, as well as the cheapest suppliers of wheat and barley.

"Have you ever seen such wonderful food? Look at those baskets filled with grapes and those pots overflowing with olives," Aleesha called out to her mother.

The time passed quickly and, before Aleesha knew it, the sun began to set into the hills around them. Though the island was much smaller than the city of Jerusalem, it reminded Aleesha of home. She had grown so tired of the desert and the never ending sight of sand.

"It is time to go back," Ima told her daughter.

"I wish we could stay here a little longer," Aleesha said

as she slowly gathered all the things they had bought and began tying them up for the walk back to the boat.

The group took their time as they boarded the boat that took them across the Nile and back to their horses. On land again, they rode slowly towards their campsite, the moon and stars guiding their way.

But when they reached the top of the hill overlooking their caravan, they realized something was terribly wrong. The tents were in shambles and the members of their group who had been left behind were running around in complete confusion. The group raced down the hill to their campsite, where Benyamin was rounding up the loose animals.

"The camp was raided," Benyamin called out to Noam, who had been to Elephantine with Aleesha and her mother.

"And the Ark?" Noam screamed back.

"It is gone!" wailed Benyamin.

* * *

Chapter Fourteen
THE ARK

ALEESHA AND HER FAMILY WORKED throughout the night cleaning up the campsite and sorting through their belongings. Only when everything was back in place did Aleesha turn back towards her own tent. As she got close to her family's desert home, she could see her father standing at the side, looking out into the desert.

"Who has the Ark, Abba?" Aleesha asked, as she walked over to her father. "Is it Jeroboam's people? Did they follow us here?"

"No, King Solomon has the Ark now. I sent the map of Elephantine to King Solomon's army before we left Jerusalem, in case Jeroboam's men followed us," Baruch said to his daughter.

"When Joseph sent word to King Solomon that we were being followed, he sent his army to Elephantine to take the Ark out of harm's way," Baruch said.

"So who raided our tents?" Aleesha asked.

"Jeroboam and his men came into our tents soon after King Solomon's army had already left with the Ark,"

Baruch said.

"Will King Solomon bring the Ark back to us, so that we can keep it in Ethiopia?" Aleesha asked.

"Maybe," Baruch said hesitantly. "But it doesn't really matter who has the Ark as long as you remember what it holds inside."

"I know it holds the Ten Commandments. But won't we forget what those commandments mean if we don't have the Ark to guide us?" asked Aleesha. It was hard to imagine living in a new place without the Ark to remind them of their past.

"No, Aleesha. We don't need the Ark to guide us. It's important to understand that if we spend our lives looking for the Ark, we will have missed the importance of its contents," Baruch said.

"But what about the tablets inside? Aren't they important?" Aleesha asked, referring to the slabs of stone on which the Ten Commandments were written and passed down by Moses to the priests. The rules inscribed on the tablets guided the people of Israel and their priests.

"Yes, they are important," Baruch said. "But have you ever wondered why the broken tablets are also inside the Ark?"

"What do you mean?" Aleesha asked.

"The broken tablets are there to remind us that it is wrong to think that the tablets themselves are more important than what is written on them," Baruch answered.

"I'm confused, Abba," replied Aleesha.

"Long ago, in the Sinai desert, the people of Israel had given up hope. They didn't believe in their leader, Moses, and turned to someone else to guide them. When Moses finally returned with the first set of stone tablets, he was so angry that he dropped the stones and they broke. But the people were given a second chance and Moses brought them the second set of tablets."

"The broken tablets remind us that people can make mistakes. But it's important to come to terms with our mistakes. You see, the tablets and the rules that are on them don't mean anything by themselves. The tablets can be broken and become worthless. It is what we make of them that matters," Baruch said. "This is why we need to study."

"I think I understand, Abba. By themselves, the words are meaningless. It's the studying of them that is important," Aleesha said.

"Yes, exactly," Baruch added. "The Ark and its commandments lie in the minds and hearts of anyone who wants to understand what they mean. Only study of the commandments can truly unlock its mysteries."

"And are its mysteries open for me as well?" Aleesha asked.

"Of course," Baruch said.

"Even though I'm a girl?" Aleesha asked.

"Yes, even though you're a girl," Baruch repeated. "You know our ways. The boys are the ones who are obliged to study and serve in the Temple. But, Aleesha, I see how important these things are for you. And I promise you that in Ethiopia you will be included in our study groups from now on.

"Besides, you already have a beautiful jewel that will reveal some of the mysteries of the world to you, if you let it," Baruch added.

"What do you mean?" Aleesha asked.

"Don't you have the emerald from the breastplate that was on the Ark?" Baruch asked.

"You know I have the emerald?" Aleesha asked, shocked.

"Yes," Baruch said. "I was in the Temple the night you went in. If I had stopped you, you would have been heard by the other priests. I knew that you could have been killed by the guards for going into the Temple.

"And you didn't tell anyone?" asked Aleesha.

"How could I? What father would betray his daughter? I stayed quiet and watched how you tried, in your own way, to come to terms with what you did," Baruch said.

"Is the Ark damaged because of what I did?" Aleesha asked.

"The Ark can never be damaged, as long as people believe in what it holds inside," Baruch said.

"I wanted to tell you about the plot I overheard and I didn't know how to make you believe me," Aleesha tried to explain. "I knew that you wouldn't doubt my story if you saw the emerald. But then the man in the brown tunic was killed and I thought you might suspect that the emerald had something to do with it. I really did want to return the emerald, only I never could find the right time." The words poured out of her with relief as she finally told her father everything.

"I know that you meant well, Aleesha," Baruch said, quietly.

"You must believe me, Abba, when I say that I promise to return the emerald one day," Aleesha said.

"I'm not sure that you will ever be able to return the emerald in your lifetime," Baruch said.

"Will we never go home again, Abba?" Aleesha asked.

"I don't think so," Baruch said quietly to his daughter. "Our new home will be in Ethiopia."

* * *

Chapter Fifteen
HABASH

ONCE THEY LEFT ELEPHANTINE and the Nile River behind them, the days seemed to get much hotter. Everyone began to watch the water levels in their gourds even closer. As their food supplies dwindled they began to worry. Without the Ark to guide them, many in the group were beginning to wonder if they shouldn't turn back. As they traveled through Egypt and Nubia, Aleesha's father spent each evening convincing his group to continue on towards Ethiopia.

Aleesha worried about what it would be like to arrive in a strange place. She wondered how they would be received and whether they would be welcomed. Along the way, she thought about the home she had left in Jerusalem and missed the hustle of the market and the warmth of her bed. As they traveled from town to town, no one paid them much attention, and even though she had her family and friends around her, Aleesha was feeling very lonely.

But when they finally made it, Aleesha could barely believe her eyes. Hundreds of people had gathered to greet

Prince Menelik and his fellow travelers to celebrate their arrival. Aleesha didn't have time to think about missing Jerusalem because the festivals lasted for weeks after the little group arrived in Axum, the capital of Habash, which was the name for Ethiopia in their ancient language. People walked for days from villages throughout the land to sing and dance in the streets of the capital, where the queen had prepared a feast for everyone to share. Servants from Sheba's palace gave out food and drink. Roasted lamb cooked in pits. Lentil stew was dished out from huge boiling pots. Women distributed fresh fruits from the baskets they carried on their heads. Men poured out different kinds of nectars and ales into cups.

Aleesha walked through the streets of Axum with Ruth, as she tried to get used to the strange language spoken by the people. They navigated their way through the crowds of women coming into town with baskets of wheat and fresh sheep's wool to sell in the market. In the center of town, women sat in a small circle with their wares of fresh goods. To one side of them, a caravan of camels rested, their knees tucked under their bodies. Their owner stood nearby, negotiating a sale price with a purchaser for one of the finest in his herd. On the other side of the road, women sold fresh chickens and eggs, calling out their prices to everyone who passed.

"We'll have to learn this new language quickly, or

we'll never be able to buy anything in this market," Aleesha joked with Ruth, as they walked arm in arm towards their new homes.

"I guess we're here for good," Ruth said with a sigh.

"Don't worry, it won't be long before we'll feel at home here," Aleesha replied.

In the evening, Prince Menelik brought all the families from Jerusalem into Queen Sheba's palace to meet his mother. Aleesha looked at the queen she had heard so much about. She was dressed in beautiful robes embroidered with gold and silver threads. In her braided hair, she wore a crown filled with red and green jewels. Her eyes sparkled even brighter than the many bracelets she wore on her arms. It was hard to look away because Sheba was so beautiful. When it was Aleesha's turn to greet the monarch, she bowed down to the ground and the queen smiled at her warmly.

"Come back tomorrow. The queen wants to speak with you," one of Sheba's guards whispered to Aleesha.

The next day, Aleesha woke up early. She spent a long time bathing in the river, brushing her hair and then scrubbing her teeth with a twig cut from a local evergreen shrub that the children in the market had given her. She wanted to look just right for her visit with the queen.

"I have heard a great deal about you," the regal Queen

Sheba said, when Aleesha arrived. Although no one in Ethiopia spoke Hebrew, the queen had learned it during her long visit with King Solomon in Jerusalem.

"And I have heard a great deal about you," Aleesha said, bowing.

"I understand that you want to study like a scholar and learn to write like a scribe," the queen said.

"Oh, yes," Aleesha said excitedly.

"You know, I like those kinds of girls," the queen said, smiling.

"Really?" Aleesha responded.

"I have a feeling that you and I will become good friends," Sheba said laughingly, as she placed her arm around Aleesha's shoulder. Together they walked through the marbled hallways to a room in the palace where hundreds of books lined the walls and scholars sat at long tables studying.

Aleesha now knew that, even though she would always miss her home in Jerusalem, she would find a way to be happy in Ethiopia.

* * *

Part Two

The Horn of Africa

Ethiopia, July 1984

Chapter One
DEBRITU

"INCREDIBLE," 14-YEAR-OLD DEBRITU WHISPERED as she stood by the door of the *gojjo,* the mud and straw thatched hut where she lived with her two younger brothers and their grandparents. Debritu looked out into the sky, shielding her eyes from the sun with her open hand. She watched as a flock of birds flew out of the trees. The loud roar of an airplane filled the air before Debritu could actually see it. The noise was becoming familiar to Debritu. Over the past few weeks so many planes had flown by that she had learned to expect the silver machines zooming across the sky.

"Come on outside, Debritu, or you'll miss it," her 12-year-old brother, Ferdu, called as he ran out of their grandparents' house, out to the dirt road.

Within minutes, all the children of the village had gathered in the dirt road just outside their small cluster of huts. From the window, Debritu watched the other children laugh and run as fast as they could, as they followed the course of the plane from the ground. Sometimes Ferdu and his friends followed for miles, before the plane disappeared into the clouds that hung low on the hills. Other times, the children would return home, disappointed, because the only thing they could see was a smoky trail that eventually faded into the sky.

Dero-woha, the tiny village where Debritu lived, was nestled into the Ethiopian highlands, southwest of the ancient city of Axum and northwest of the modern Ethiopian capital of Addis Ababa. The village of 50 Jewish families was about a two-hour walk to the town of Gedebye and less than a day's journey away from Gondar, the nearest city. Debritu sometimes traveled by bus along the bumpy road into Gondar with her grandfather, when he went to buy tools for his work. Compared to Gedebye, Gondar seemed like such a busy place with cars, trucks and buses connecting towns and cities all over Ethiopia.

At that time, Ethiopia stretched from the Red Sea in the north to the country of Kenya in the south. Somalia and Djibouti framed its eastern borders, and Sudan lay to the west. At school, Debritu learned that the entire region juts into the Indian Ocean from the northeast side of Africa, curving north toward Arabia like a pointed horn, giving their part of the continent its nickname, the Horn of Africa.

Debritu's village stood at the foot of the Semien Mountains. All around Dero-woha, the hills grew taller and steeper, until they soared into some of the highest peaks in the area. Ras Dejen, the fourth-highest mountain in Africa, stood with its peak in the clouds at 4,000 meters. Baboons, ibex and wolves roamed through the wide river valleys and over the rocky, shrub-covered slopes. Up above, white-billed starlings floated across the sky alongside black-feathered ravens. Recently, the Ethiopian government started sending airplanes filled with soldiers to fight the rebels who hid in the northern hills and mountains. It seemed as if a day never went by without a plane flying overhead.

Since the late 1970s, Ethiopia was ruled by a cruel and powerful dictator, Mengistu Haile Mariam, who had come to power by overthrowing Haile Selassie, the last of the Ethiopian emperors. Haile Selassie had claimed to be a descendent of Menelik, the son of King Solomon and the Queen of Sheba. In the late 19th and early 20th centuries, Haile Selassie, who called himself the Lion of Judah, proudly wore Solomon's ring that had been given to his son, Prince Menelik, and passed down through the generations. Emperor Haile Selassie and his immediate predecessors had spread the Amharic-speaking Empire further than it had ever gone before. They had conquered many neighboring peoples, expanding the borders of Ethiopia.

But when the emperor was overthrown by Mengistu's

armed forces, many of the non-Amharic people that formed Ethiopia began to seek independence. It didn't take long before many different groups of rebels began to challenge the government. In the east, there was an Oromo liberation movement and in the southeast there was a Somali separatist movement centered in the Ogaden desert. Near Axum, the Tigrayans were fighting the government. And just north of that, the Eritreans had long been fighting to separate from Ethiopia and form their own independent state. In their quest for power, the rebels also fought amongst themselves.

The city of Gondar was a perfect launching spot for Mengistu's soldiers to attack the rebels. By 1984, the Semien Mountains were filled with rebels and soldiers, with each group facing off against each other and the central army, which tried to confront them all.

As the plane passed overhead, Debritu wondered whether to leave her chores and join the children in the road. Though she was older, she too wanted to join in the fun. But there was work to do and she would have to stay and finish. She could just imagine the boys arguing with each other about which one would be the first to fly an airplane.

"When I grow up, I'm going to fly an airplane," Ferdu had declared the last time an airplane passed over their little village. Debritu knew that in Ethiopia, Beyta

Israel boys were never taught to fly airplanes. Ferdu cried when she told him that he would never be able to become a pilot.

Inside the *gojjo*, Debritu turned back to her work. She poked at the sleepy coals that glowed warmly by the door of their hut. Branches and twigs were piled outside their *gojjo* for Debritu to add to the fire when it burned too low. Debritu knew that without a burning fire there would be nothing to prevent wild animals from roaming into their home. At the back of the *gojjo*, Debritu could hear the steady bang of a stone hitting a rock as her grandmother pounded cloves of garlic into a smooth paste. Quickly, Debritu looked around to see what her baby brother was up to.

"Get away from that basket!" Debritu suddenly yelled. It was too late. Her three-year-old brother, Asefa, had managed to pull himself up against a tall straw basket filled with beans. Before Debritu could reach her brother, Asefa had toppled the basket over, scattering the beans all around.

"Oh, you silly boy," Debritu said with a laugh, as she scooped him up into her arms to give him a kiss. Once she put Asefa safely down next to her grandmother, Debritu began picking up the beans. As she worked, she thought again about Ferdu and his desire to become a pilot.

"Why are we Jews different from everyone else?"

Debritu asked her grandmother, whom she called Imita, the Amharic word for grandmother. Debritu and her family spoke Amharic, one of the area's several Semitic languages.

"What do you mean?" Imita answered gently.

"Why can't a Falasha boy become a pilot for instance?" Debritu asked, cynically. She didn't like the term Falasha, even though villagers in the area called them by that name.

"Because that is the way things are here in Ethiopia," Imita answered. "There are Amhara and Tigrayan farmers. There are the proud Afar herdsmen and the Oromo-speaking cattle breeders. We, the Beyta Israel, who are called Falashas by our neighbours, are the potters, weavers and blacksmiths."

"Can't things change?" Debritu asked.

"Debritu, now is not the time to solve the world's problems. Now is the time to get ready for *Sanbat*," Imita said with a sigh.

In fact, Debritu was right. There were a lot of things that the Beyta Israel people couldn't do. In her area, for example, they weren't allowed to own land for farming. It was almost impossible for them to go to university or hold government jobs. The list of things they couldn't do sometimes seemed endless.

"Why do they call us Falashas?" Debritu asked her

grandmother. "Falasha means 'stranger.' But I feel just as Ethiopian as everyone else. Why don't they call us 'Beyta Israel' like our elders do?"

"Falasha is what they have called us here for years. You must accept it and not take what other people say so seriously," Imita said. This daughter of her eldest daughter never seemed at rest with the old ways. Instead she asked many questions and was always looking for answers.

"How can I ignore everyone? All the people in the nearby villages treat us differently, as if we're not as good as they are. It isn't fair," Debritu responded, feeling the anger rise up from her stomach to her cheeks.

Debritu knew that Jews had lived in Ethiopia for centuries. Because they weren't allowed to own land, many Beyta Israel families rented small parcels of farmable land from property owners who lived far away. They had also become ironsmiths, weavers and potters, and sold their goods to support their families.

"You and your questions," Imita said to her grand-daughter, trying to sound stern. "Debritu, please get back to your chores. We need to get ready for the Sabbath."

* * *

Chapter Two
THE BEYTA ISRAEL PEOPLE

FRIDAY WAS A VERY BUSY TIME IN DERO-WOHA. In order to get their laundry washed, their firewood gathered, their water pots filled, their food prepared, and their homes cleaned before *Sanbat*, the men, women and children of Dero-woha got up an hour earlier on Fridays. From first thing in the morning, the whole village worked hard so that everything would be ready on time. There was a lot to do before the Sabbath, which began before sundown.

Debritu knew that once the sun faded away into the night, their day of rest would begin. The Sabbath, which was called *Sanbat* in Amharic, was the most holy day of the week for the Jews of Ethiopia. For centuries, the Beyta Israel observed this day with great care so that it was truly a day of rest. All the weavers, tailors, carpenters, potters, blacksmiths and farmers would work very hard all week long. But on the Sabbath, everyone, the well-to-do and the very poor, the young and the old, knew that they must rest.

The Beyta Israel people lived in the small villages that were sprinkled throughout the northern hills of Ethiopia. Each community was built carefully into the Ethiopian hillsides isolated from each other. In fact, the Beyta Israel people had lived in isolation from the rest of the Jewish world for hundreds of years. For the longest time, these Ethiopian Jews did not know of any other Jews. They believed that the Jews outside of Ethiopia had been killed, scattered or exiled to Babylonia during raids on Jerusalem over 2,500 years ago. Their elders had taught them that the responsibility to preserve the books of the ancient priests had been handed down to them through the generations from King Solomon's time. They told stories about temple priests and their families who left Jerusalem and traveled through Egypt and Sudan to Ethiopia.

For Debritu and her family, the Sabbath began when the *kessotch*, the priests or elders, rang their bells, calling the villagers to prayer. Debritu made sure that their best clothes were freshly cleaned and set aside for herself and her brothers. Once they were all washed and dressed, Debritu tied Asefa on her back. Then, she and Ferdu walked, hand in hand, just behind their grandparents, to the village synagogue. Their little house of worship stood in the center of the village, with a little Star of David that stood proudly on the very tip of the mud and straw-thatched roof. Inside the hut, another Star of David was painted in the center of the peaked roof. Underneath the star, the men, women and children of Dero-woha would say prayers and think about Jerusalem.

Later, Debritu ate the Sabbath dinner with her brothers and their grandparents. It was a special evening for every family. On this night, their grandfather would spend his time at home, relaxing with his family. Together, inside their *gojjo*, Debritu and her family shared stories about Noah, Abraham, Sarah and Isaac. On the Sabbath, Debritu and her family were not allowed to gather firewood or work in any way. Instead they spent the day resting and praying. When she and her brothers went to bed after the Sabbath evening meal, her grandfather went back to the house of prayer for the rest of the night.

The next morning, Debritu returned to the house of prayer with her grandmother. She loved listening to the *kessotch* recite the Ten Commandments in *Ge'ez*, an ancient Semitic language. Although the *kessotch* always translated their prayers from *Ge'ez* to their own language, Amharic, so that the people could understand the words, Debritu liked listening to the rhythm of *Ge'ez*, a language that made her think of a distant land, long ago. Once the prayers were finished, the *kessotch* would bless the large loaves of bread that were brought to the house of prayer by all the families. The bread was then sliced carefully and the center pieces were put aside for the *kessotch* and elders in the village. The rest of the bread was passed around to the villagers, and everyone would eat, drink and rest until late in the afternoon.

The elders taught the people that long ago and far away, in the ancient land of Israel, the stories of the Torah, or the *Orit* as the Beyta Israel called it, took place. Made up of the Five Books of Moses, as well as the books of the Prophets, the *Orit* held the stories that bound the Ethiopian Jewish communities together. They believed that the *Orit* was given to them by Moses in the Sinai desert, along with the Ten Commandments.

Beyta Israel traditions were passed on through the generations since the days of old. Rituals were led by the elders and priests. Parents taught their children how to celebrate the holy days, how to say blessings over their food and how to immerse themselves in the river nearby in order to purify their bodies. Debritu and her brothers were taught to remember the city of Jerusalem where a great Temple had once stood. On the morning of the holy day of *Sigd*, a day of fasting for the whole Ethiopian Jewish community, Debritu's people walked together to the nearest mountaintop and read from the *Orit*. From the peaks of the mountain, they would recall their traditions and voice their desire to return to Jerusalem one day.

Chapter Three
EMAMA AND ABBAT

DEBRITU'S GRANDFATHER, whom the children called Ayat, spent almost every morning in his iron-smith's yard making farming tools. Sometimes he made plows, sometimes hoes. The rest of his time was spent negotiating payments with farmers who came in for new tools.

Debritu had lived with her grandparents for long enough to know that during the busy harvest time, it was better to stay out of her grandfather's way. Everyone knew of Ayat's talents as an ironsmith. All the farmers in the area bought their tools from the man they called the Falasha with the magical hands. When he wasn't busy working in his shop forging farming equipment, Ayat liked to travel up and down the hillsides to watch his tools being used. Sometimes he watched the oxen as they pulled the ploughs he had made to see if there was any way to improve the sharp blades that turned up the clumpy soil. Other times he would chat with the farmers to hear how their harvests were going.

98

Ayat was one of the most well respected men in the village. His travels allowed him to learn what was happening in the region. As soon as Ayat came back from his journeys, he would call a meeting with the elders in Derowoha to let them know what he had learned. All the Ethiopian Jews who lived in the hillside villages relied on Debritu's grandfather to keep them informed about what was happening in the rest of the world.

At least twice a week, Debritu would watch men in uniforms, carrying rifles at their sides, ride horses into their little village to have coffee with Ayat. The men were so mean looking, Debritu wondered how her grandfather could sit with them. After they left, Debritu's grandfather would sigh with relief and complain bitterly that he had to bribe them, to make sure that the army would stay away from their village. The army had been raiding villages all around the countryside for draftable men, and since Debritu's father had been taken by soldiers, Ayat gave whatever spare cash he had to army officials, so that the people in his village could sleep safely at night.

It had been four years since her father, whom they called Abbat, had been forced into the Ethiopian army to fight the rebels. Under the dictator, President Mengistu, the Ethiopian army often raided the towns and villages, forcing the men between the ages of 18 and 30 to join them. Those who were fortunate were warned and hid in the bush before the soldiers arrived. The unfortunate ones were taken away by force.

Debritu remembered the night that the soldiers had come into their home and taken her father away. She recalled how her mother, Emama, had wailed and pleaded with the soldiers, begging them to leave her husband alone. They all watched as Abbat struggled with the men in their uniforms.

"The fighting stops now or one of you will get hurt," the soldier said, pointing his gun at Ferdu. Debritu quickly pulled her brother into the house, as the soldiers took her father away. The two children sat huddled together, inside, until there was complete quiet. Then they went outside and sat beside their mother, who sat on the ground, her head in her hands.

"I'm scared," Ferdu whispered to his mother when she began to cry. But Debritu didn't think that Emama was listening. Emama seemed totally unaware of the children sitting beside her as she cried for most of the night. Debritu had a strange feeling that more than her father had been taken that night, and she too became afraid. But for the sake of their family, Debritu would have to learn to hide it from Ferdu.

After their father's disappearance, her mother began to change. For days, she stayed in bed refusing to get up. Finally, she gave birth to Asefa and the neighboring women, friends and relatives from the village, came by to take care of her and her children.

"Bring her chicken *wat*," some had suggested when Emama didn't seem to be getting any better.

"No, plain porridge," others advised.

The women filled the *gojjo* with food and drink and tried to bring happy news. But Emama remained in bed and responded to their questions with short and simple answers. As time passed, she seemed to get weaker.

"Eat just a little more," Debritu would plead with her mother every day, as she tried to get her to swallow just a bit of porridge. But after a spoonful went into her mouth, the gaunt woman would turn away and face the walls of their small thatched *gojjo*.

In the meantime, the beans in the food basket began to dwindle and Debritu worried about how they would fill their stomachs each night. Debritu spent the day taking care of the newborn and watching over her mother. Sometimes, Ferdu would go out in the mornings to help the shepherds tend their cattle and sheep, so that he could bring home a little bit of milk.

Debritu learned to visit the neighboring homes with Asefa swaddled on her back. She waited outside her uncles' and aunts' doors for food to bring home for her mother, herself and her brothers. Whenever she had extra time, she went out to pull the weeds out of the fields, for a bit of wheat in payment. And each night, Debritu would sing to her mother and help her sit up so that she could eat just a little bit.

Once, while Debritu waited for food to take home, she overheard her aunt talking to a woman visiting from another village.

"Nothing seems to help. The women in the village have tried everything," her aunt said.

"Maybe it's malaria," the other woman responded.

"Yes, it could be malaria. Or maybe she's trapped in the dark part of her mind," said her aunt.

"She probably needs a doctor from the city to remove the evil that has caught her," her uncle responded.

"It is time for the children to move in with their grandparents," the aunt and uncle agreed.

Debritu walked home that evening, with tears in her eyes, a few eggs in her pocket and enough wheat and sorghum for herself and her brothers. Rain, which was beginning to fall more sporadically than usual, was pouring down around her and the red mud squished through her toes. Her feet sank into the road with every step. She walked slowly, worried about what was ahead. Debritu decided that, no matter what happened, she would be strong for her brothers. Otherwise, Ferdu might decide to run away and look for their father, and there would be no way to keep the family together.

A few days later, her grandfather came to their home wearing his white cotton *shemma* wrapped proudly over his shoulders. Debritu watched her grandfather lean against his long, wooden walking stick, rubbing the ivory handle as he watched her mother sleeping restlessly. "Will Emama be alright?" Debritu asked meekly, bowing her head so that her eyes looked down with respect.

"Your mother needs better care now than you can give her here," her grandfather replied.

"Emama must go to the hospital in the big city, Addis Ababa, for awhile. You and your brothers will come to live with me and your grandmother," he announced to Debritu.

That evening, Debritu sat beside her mother's bed. Debritu told her mother all about her fears and worries. Her mother did not respond. When she was finished, Debritu looked at her mother with love and concern.

"Don't worry, Emama. I won't disappoint you. I'll be strong and never let anyone see just how scared I am. I promise that I will take care of Ferdu and Asefa. But you have to promise to get better and come home soon," Debritu whispered to her mother as she kissed her tired face. "And please don't forget us."

* * *

Chapter Four
A NEW HOME

I T DIDN'T TAKE LONG FOR DEBRITU to gather their few belongings and walk the short distance down the dirt path with her brothers. They crossed three fields of grass before they came to the edge of the village where her grandparents lived. Debritu and her brothers put their little bundles down in their grandparents' mud and straw-thatched *gojjo*, so similar to the home they had just left behind. From the doorway of her new home, Debritu watched Ayat go into the adjacent big stone house with the corrugated tin roof.

Ayat and his wife lived in the biggest property in their little village. Besides the *gojjo* where they slept, they had two other round huts and one stone building, all enclosed by a wood fence. Ayat owned goats, sheep, cows and chickens, which he kept in his little compound. Debritu felt so proud of her grandfather. She knew that he was an important man and that everyone respected him.

"Debritu, you will help your grandmother in the house and watch over Asefa. Ferdu, you can help feed the chickens and milk the cows," Ayat instructed the children.

"You are allowed in the two smaller *gojjos*. But children must stay out of the stone house," Ayat announced firmly, as he sent Ferdu to tie their horses into the corral where the animals were kept. "The stone house is where I receive my important guests," Ayat explained.

I wonder what is in that stone house, Debritu thought, while she tied up the horses and observed the cows and sheep that her grandfather owned.

As she unpacked their things, she wished that her white cotton smock wasn't so tattered, that Asefa's pants weren't all so short, and that Ferdu's shirt had at least one button left. She wondered if Ferdu felt as embarrassed as she did. But the truth was that Ferdu never really seemed concerned about how he looked. He always seemed happy, as long as he could play. Before too long, Ferdu was off with a group of his old friends, pulling a log onto a big boulder so they could seesaw up and down.

Once Debritu had unpacked their belongings, she needed to visit her best friend, Alemitu, who lived close by, to tell her the news. She told her about their mother's departure to Addis Ababa and their move into their grandparents' house.

"Are you going to stay there forever?" her friend asked.

"I don't know," Debritu replied. "I hope not."

"Don't worry, I'm sure your Emama will be home soon," said Alemitu, reassuringly.

"I hope so," Debritu answered.

"Let's go tell everyone about your move," Alemitu said, trying to cheer up her friend.

And they ran to the well, where the young girls gathered when they finished their chores.

In their new home, Debritu gathered the firewood, helped her grandmother with the cooking and watched over Asefa. If she finished her work quickly and put Asefa down for a nap, she would have more time to explore her new surroundings.

Before long, she knew each one of the houses owned by her grandfather. Despite Ayat's warning, Debritu found the stone house the most fun to explore, with its storage rooms filled with honey, butter, sugar and *teff*. Downstairs, the room had a table and chairs for the elders to discuss their affairs.

Debritu would sometimes sit on the wooden chairs and force Ferdu to pretend that he was a government official. "You say that you need more *teff* to feed your soldiers," Debritu would say sternly, as she pretended to pour Ferdu more beer and passed him imaginary plates of cake.

"Well, I'm sure we can handle that," Debritu would declare.

Before too long, Ferdu grew tired of Debritu's pretend

games and made his way outside to play soccer with his friends.

Soon Ayat announced that Ferdu and Debritu would begin school once again. Debritu was thrilled. Even though most girls in Dero-woha weren't allowed to go to school, Emama had insisted that all her children learn to read and write. Debritu and Ferdu had been registered in the nearby school as soon as they were old enough. But when their father was taken into the army, Debritu and her brother had stopped going to classes and Debritu wasn't sure whether she would ever go back.

"Who will watch over Asefa?" Debritu asked, confused. One part of her was excited. Another part was worried about her baby brother.

"Imita will watch over Asefa, while you are in school," Ayat said, adding that Debritu and Ferdu would need new clothes before school started. "My grandchildren will not go to school in rags," Ayat declared. Debritu could barely contain her excitement. Even though she still missed her own parents, her grandparents' house was beginning to feel more like her own home.

The very next market day, Ayat took the three children into Gedebye, the closest town, to buy a new skirt for Debritu and a new pair of pants for Ferdu. The two older children also got new shoes, so that they wouldn't have to walk barefoot to school. Even Asefa, who was too young for school, got a new pair of shorts and a white cotton shirt. The children returned to Dero-woha, happier than they had been in a very long time.

Once school started, Debritu got up before the sun, prepared breakfast and lunch for herself and Ferdu, and met the few other girls from her village who were also allowed to go to school. As the pink sun rose over the green Ethiopian hills, the girls walked together down the dirt road that passed by the villages and fields, until they came to the school. The wood building with 10 windows standing side by side, where all the children from the area studied until high school, stretched along an empty field.

The girls walked together, joking as they passed the fields of *teff* and wheat, holding hands as they hurried past the occasional cluster of huts that dotted the hillside. The girls never walked to or from school alone. They knew that they could be attacked by bandits along the way. Even worse, the nearby jumble of trees might be filled with danger. No one dared to cut through the wild shrubs and knotted acacias that stood at the edge of the school.

The children knew about the thieves and bandits that sometimes hid behind the trees. Debritu's grandmother also warned her about the rebels and soldiers that slept in the mountains, waiting to rob strangers. But most of all, Debritu worried about the jackals and hyenas that sometimes hid in the woods. Twice a day, the girls would race by the trees on their way to and from school, always staying together for protection.

"Tell us one of your stories," Alemitu would beg as they set out early each morning.

"Which story?" Debritu asked.

Debritu was usually happy to oblige with a tale. The storyteller of the group, she often retold a legend she had heard from her family. Other times, she made up something as she went along. Nothing made Debritu happier than being able to watch her words make her friends laugh and cry. Debritu knew that Alemitu loved the story about "Truth and Lies" the best.

"Wisdom, Stupidity, Truth and Lies were once the very best of friends and traveled together amongst the clouds," Debritu began. "One day, they looked down on the Earth and together they came across a beautiful baby named Menelik, who was the only child born to King Solomon and the Queen of Sheba," Debritu went on. "Lies decided that the baby should belong to him alone. So he told Wisdom and Stupidity to find King Solomon and the Queen of Sheba to warn them that the baby was alone and in danger. While Wisdom and Stupidity hurried to warn the royal couple of the danger, a great confusion settled on the land. Then Lies went to Truth and tried to persuade her that Wisdom and Stupidity were about to steal the baby and that she must warn the queen and king. But

Truth understood that something was wrong and didn't trust Lies. She refused to go. And soon the two began to fight."

"And did Lies beat Truth and get the baby?" Alemitu asked.

"No," Debritu said. "Truth and Lies struggled back and forth that day. Since then, the feud has lasted forever. And neither one has ever been able to destroy the other."

"Is that the truth?" Alemitu asked, and the girls would laugh so hard that tears rolled down their cheeks.

* * *

Chapter Five
MARKET DAY IN GEDEBYE

IT HAD BEEN CLOSE TO A YEAR since her mother had left them and Debritu thought about Emama all the time. She wondered when she would get better and come home. Even though she desperately wanted to go visit her mother in Addis Ababa, the capital was a very long distance from Dero-woha. It could take up to a week to make the trip. Sometimes weeks would go by without a word about her mother before Ayat would make the long journey and come back to report on Emama's health.

"Your mother is getting better slowly," Ayat said after each trip. But as time went on, Debritu began to wonder whether to believe him.

A few months after Debritu moved in with her grandparents and started classes, her friend Alemitu got married and stopped going to school. Debritu walked back and forth with her other friends. But she missed her best friend. On market days when school wasn't in session, Debritu joined Alemitu in selling her pottery. Together, they would walk the few miles into Gedebye. The two girls left early in the morning, each with three or four clay pots tied to their backs. Sometimes Imita let them use their mule. Then Debritu and Alemitu would tie as many pots as they could to the mule's back.

At the market, Alemitu spread a blanket down on the ground where the girls placed the pottery and they waited for buyers who came from the surrounding villages for their supplies. Since both girls loved mingling in the crowd, they would take turns selling the pots. One would watch their blanket, while the other roamed through the streets to do her family's shopping and check for new and interesting things.

When it was Debritu's turn, she scurried over to the jewelry stall where bangles, necklaces and rings were spread out for everyone to see. It was so much fun to pretend that she could afford them. *Maybe one day I'll be able to buy Emama a beautiful bracelet,* she thought, as she gingerly ran her fingers over a carved copper bangle.

"How much for that red skirt?" Without her grandmother around, she took her time looking at the jewelry and skirts and dresses laid out so nicely on blankets on the ground. Debritu loved to look at the different styles of pants and skirts that came in so many different colors. Then she went from stall to stall, remembering to buy all the things her grandmother had asked for. If she didn't hurry and get everything they needed, Imita would be annoyed.

"How much to fill my pitcher with oil?" Debritu began bargaining with a farmer. Behind him in a mud-thatched stall, his son led a camel round and round, as the pole attached to its back went up and down the well, churning the sesame seeds into oil.

"One *birr*," the farmer said.

"Don't be ridiculous, I asked for one pitcher, not two," Debritu said, remembering that her grandmother had given her five *birr* and told her that any money left over after shopping was hers to keep.

After she pretended to walk away a few times, the merchant called her back and agreed. He filled Debritu's pitcher with oil and handed her a half *birr* for change.

"A girl must know how to bargain," Imita had explained. "Otherwise she will never be able to run a home."

Debritu never tired of going into the market. Sometimes she would see Tigrayans arrive from the northwest with their colorful woven baskets to sell. Other times she saw Afar boys from the east wearing turbans and carrying sticks to keep their camels in line. As Debritu went from stall to stall, she also listened to the stories that the sellers would tell about news from their regions. "There have been too many seasons without enough rain. The crops are dying and there is less and less to eat every day," she overheard a merchant from a nearby town say.

"In the east, the herdsmen have started bringing their cattle into the farmers' fields to eat, so that the cows don't starve. There is not enough for everyone and some are beginning to go hungry," said another merchant.

"Some farmers have begun leaving their homes and families in search of food and work in Addis," the first man said.

"It doesn't help that the government and rebels continue their fighting in the countryside," the second man said. From their talk, Debritu learned that there were many different rebel groups hiding in the northern Ethiopian hills and mountains.

On the way home, Debritu began to worry. Surely, there would always be enough to eat in their little village of Dero-woha. Alemitu noticed that her friend was quiet on the road back and squeezed her hand.

"Those men don't know everything. As long as we work hard, we will have enough," Alemitu tried to reassure her.

Yet, both girls knew that over the past few months there were many signs of famine in their country. Ethiopia was constantly plagued by too little rain. The people of Ethiopia knew the dangers of famine from past experience. Without enough rain there would be no water. Without water, the animals and crops would die. And without crops and livestock, the people would starve.

Chapter Six
VISITORS

THOUGH AYAT DIDN'T WORK IN THE FIELDS, he often spent his afternoons checking on the farmers to see how their crops were doing. His many years as the only ironsmith in the area had taught him that the time to ask for payment was when the farmers brought in their harvests. That was when baskets were full of food. When the harvest was decent, villagers could breathe easier, confident that hunger wasn't immediately around the corner. But it was never easy to ask for payment, especially from the farmers in the area who worried about feeding their own families.

These days it was even harder to ask for payment. Times were tough. Most of the grown men who hadn't already been drafted into the army were forced to work on government-run communal farms. That left only the older men, the women and the young boys and girls to work in the fields.

"How can I expect them to pay for my tools when they barely have enough food for themselves?" Ayat would ask his wife when he came home. The crops had begun to shrink and people were beginning to wonder what would happen if the men didn't come back. Starvation was the village's greatest fear.

At home, Ayat was often frustrated with a situation that didn't seem to be getting any easier. After a day in town looking for payment, Debritu sometimes heard him ask Imita how he would feed his own family, if he gave away his tools for nothing.

Debritu was wondering if things could get any worse, when she caught sight of two figures on horseback in the far distance, making their way to their little mountain village. The blurry dust cloud moved quickly as it wound its way through the green fields that spotted the red and black Ethiopian valley. At the speed they were going, they would arrive in the village just before dark.

Who are these visitors and why are they coming so late in the day? Debritu asked herself, as she finished her evening chores outside the *gojjo*. It was very unusual to have relatives or friends coming for a visit before nightfall. And Ethiopians from the neighboring villages rarely came to socialize with the Beyta Israel. Watching them approach made her nervous inside.

Debritu was soon joined by Imita in looking out at the approaching horsemen. "These are not from our people," her grandmother said under her breath.

"What do you mean?" asked Debritu.

"This will not be a good visit," she muttered, as she rewrapped her shawl around her shoulders.

"Why won't this be a good visit?" Debritu asked as she emptied the last bits of wheat into the basket. But her grandmother barely looked at Debritu, as she ordered, "Hurry up and get the water. Don't go to the well. It's too far. Get the water from the river." Then Imita turned and went into the house.

From the tone of her grandmother's voice, Debritu knew that she had better hurry. She grabbed the two clay pots from inside the *gojjo* and ran down the grassy hill to the stream that flowed near the edge of their village. Fortunately, the streams were still gurgling with muddy, brownish water that tumbled over the pebbles and rocks. In the dry season, which lasted from October to January, the creeks and river beds often dried up and the line for water at the well was so long that it sometimes took half the day to get what she needed.

When she returned, Debritu was out of breath and her grandmother was waiting outside the *gojjo*. Debritu could see that Imita was worried.

"Get the water ready," Imita said. "We will wash their feet together."

"Really?" Debritu asked, surprised. "You're going to wash the visitors' feet?"

Her grandmother interrupted, "Just do what you're told."

It's very unusual for Imita to wash the feet of visiting strangers, Debritu thought. Normally she herself poured the water over the feet of visitors.

Debritu had just enough time to get the washing bowls ready and fill the pitchers with water before she heard the horsemen arrive at her grandfather's home. Quietly, she slipped behind the *gojjo* to wait for her grandmother's call.

She could hear the strangers getting off their horses and the sound of angry voices. By the time her grandmother called her, she nervously went out to help take off their leather shoes and pour the cool water over their dirty feet.

It was hard not to look up at the faces of the strangers, but she knew that if they caught her looking at them, they would accuse the girl of being rude. From the corner of her eyes, Debritu could see that they had wrapped their white cotton *shemmas* over their heads and shoulders.

They're probably farmers who live between Dero-woha and Gedebye, Debritu thought.

Imita beckoned for them to sit down on the benches she had prepared for them and Debritu put the bowl down. Together, Debritu and Imita took off their black leather shoes and poured the cool water over their muddy feet. As they washed, Debritu could see knives tucked into the belts of the strangers.

"We're here to see the ironsmith," one man said, once they were done washing.

"And your knives? Can they stay outside?" Imita asked.

"There won't be trouble here today," the other man said. "But the ironsmith must know we mean business."

Imita sighed as she led the two men into the main house and closed the door behind them. When the visitors were settled into the main house with her grandparents, Debritu grabbed Asefa and ran as fast as she could to her favorite uncle's house. She needed some answers.

* * *

Chapter Seven
BIRUK'S STORIES

DEBRITU'S FAVORITE UNCLE, Biruk, lived with his wife, Enanu, in a small thatched hut at the other end of Dero-woha. Biruk was too old for the army, but everyone was worried that he too might be taken away to work on one of the government farms. Even though their *gojjo* was small, it was always warm and welcoming. Many people from the village came here in the evenings to listen to Biruk tell stories.

At the side of their *gojjo*, Biruk had a box of books with pictures of faraway places and different-looking people. Biruk knew how to read many different languages, including English. He was the only one who had left the village, to study in a country called England. When he came back, Biruk told the villagers how people in England lived and worked in buildings made of brick and concrete, many of which rose high up into the sky.

From the moment he began his tales, both young and old would listen to him describe new worlds. He always made them think about things in different ways, beyond their own experiences and traditions.

"Strangers have come to Ayat's house," Debritu said to her uncle, out of breath from her brisk walk with Asefa on her back. She paid no attention to her young cousins who were beginning their evening meal outside the *gojjo*.

"Calm down and eat, little *tota*," her aunt Enanu said. "When you have some food in you, we'll talk."

Tota, "monkey" in Amharic, was a term of endearment Enanu used for Debritu, because she said her niece was always jumping from tree to tree, as if the branches were on fire.

"But, they have knives . . . . ," Debritu went on impatiently.

"Take a plate of food and eat outside with your cousins. I want to finish talking with your aunt," Biruk said to his niece.

Debritu sighed. It was clearly no use arguing with her aunt and uncle. She took a piece of *injara*, unrolled it on a plate and went to stand next to her aunt's fire, where a pot of *wat* was simmering. The chunks of chicken, slivers of hot peppers and dots of lentils bobbed in the boiling pot. Debritu mixed it, before she ladled a spoon of the stew onto her plate. Once her *injara* was covered with the *wat*, she crouched outside the door with her cousins and watched them rip off bits of *injara,* with which they pinched chunks of *wat* to put into their mouths.

As Debritu began eating, she thought about the stories her uncle had told.

Sometimes he told stories of clever animals that used tricks to solve their problems. Other times, he told of great kings and wise queens from the past. For hours after each story, Debritu would think about Biruk's tales and how things could have been resolved differently. It was from him she had learned to tell her own stories.

Many nights, Debritu would sit with the men and women of her village, tired after their long day's work. She would sip the sweet coffee Enanu made for all their guests, while Biruk told his stories under the starry sky. Debritu always felt good listening to the monkeys chattering in the distance as they settled into their treetop beds while the crickets chirped from their blades of grass.

Before Biruk began his stories, Enanu would burn incense and spread grass out for everyone to sit on in the traditional Ethiopian way. It was meant as a way to remind everyone that nature was always a part of their lives. And while her uncle told his stories, Enanu would make sure that the clay cups were always full of coffee, and that the ceramic bowls were filled with enough freshly popped corn for everyone to eat.

Sometimes Biruk would tell stories about the powerful King Solomon. "His wisdom was known far and wide, and his courts of law were famous throughout his kingdom," Biruk would start.

"But most of all, everyone knew about the Temple he built for his Ark of the Covenant. They knew about the gold, the silver and the ivory that covered the walls and ceilings of his Temple. They heard about the jewels and gems that were sent to this wise king from every part of the world, and they knew about the Ark where the stone tablets were kept. All the people in the kingdom cherished those tablets, because on them were written the Ten Commandments, the laws of the land. Evil kings and warriors went to war to capture those tablets, but no one could," Biruk went on to say.

Biruk told them about King Solomon's son, Menelik, who traveled to Jerusalem and back to Ethiopia when he was a young man. When Queen Sheba died, Menelik became the emperor of Ethiopia and the ancestor of an Ethiopian dynasty. Like his father, he was known to be a very wise king and he ruled his people with great courage.

"There are people who believe that Menelik took the Ark of the Covenant with him from Jerusalem and kept it hidden here in Ethiopia," Biruk said.

"The Ark is here, in Ethiopia? Can we see it?" Debritu asked.

"No," Biruk answered. "It is believed to be hidden in Axum, the ancient city in the mountains, near the ruins of Queen Sheba's palace. Very few people, if any, have actually ever seen it. But many Ethiopians believe that the Ark is here."

"Do you believe it is here?" Debritu asked.

"I believe that the Ark is much more than just a box and that it doesn't matter where it actually is," Biruk said.

"But what is the truth?" Debritu asked, trying hard to understand her uncle.

"The truth is the way that guides us towards wisdom and righteousness," Biruk said. "The belief that takes you in that direction is the right road to follow."

Debritu loved nights spent around her uncle and aunt's fire. Here, no one told her that it wasn't a young girl's place to be so curious about everything. After a long day working, everyone was content to feel the cool night around them, sip sweet coffee and nibble on freshly popped corn, while Biruk told his stories and Debritu asked her questions.

Debritu's favorite story was about Queen Yehudit, who ruled Ethiopia hundreds of years ago. "A great war took place in northern Habash, in the kingdom of Axum," Biruk would start. "At that time, the kingdom of Axum stretched far and wide and the Beyta Israel people were led by a very strong queen, Yehudit, who came from an Israelite family. With her powerful troops, Yehudit overcame the rulers of Axum. For 40 years, Yehudit ruled over the Semien Mountains and much of the north and the

Beyta Israel prospered. No one could challenge her strength or courage as she won battle after battle for her people."

"And then one day," Biruk continued, "Yehudit decided that she must capture the Ark of the Covenant and return it to her people."

"And did she?" Debritu asked, excited at the thought of Yehudit bringing the Ark back to Jerusalem.

"Does it really matter?" Biruk asked his niece.

"What do you mean? Of course it matters," Debritu asked, confused.

"Oh little *tota*," Biruk said. "For you there are only black and white answers. But isn't it possible that each person has his or her own way of seeing things, so that there is no right and wrong? Sometimes the answers are found in the shades of gray."

"I don't understand," Debritu said.

"If we believe that the Ark was returned to Jerusalem, that would mean the Ethiopian people don't have it, and are wrong in their beliefs," Biruk said.

"But surely there is a right and a wrong," Debritu said. "Either they have the Ark or we have the Ark."

"When it comes to the traditions of a people, there is no right or wrong. The important thing is that when you follow your traditions, you also respect the beliefs of others," Biruk replied. "When you lose respect for each other, then you have chosen to travel down the wrong road."

Biruk also told stories about modern times, about groups of Beyta Israel who were making their way back to the city of Jerusalem. When Biruk talked about their bravery and strength, Debritu imagined herself courageous and bold like Queen Yehudit, overcoming the desert *shiftas*. She dreamed of arriving at the doors of the beautiful Temple in Jerusalem where she would be welcomed by her own people.

But today, while the strangers sat inside her grandfather's hut, her uncle and aunt weren't telling any stories. Instead they were whispering to each other while the children ate. And Debritu could tell from their faces that they were worried.

* * *

Chapter Eight
HYENAS AND BULLIES

"WHO ARE THESE STRANGERS and why are they here?" Debritu asked her uncle and aunt when they were ready to talk with her.

"There was trouble in the fields this morning," Enanu said.

"What do you mean?" Debritu asked, shaking out her straw plate.

"Early this morning your grandfather set out to Gedebye and stopped to speak to one of the Amhara farmers while the children were still playing in the fields," Enanu tried to explain.

"So what?" Debritu asked.

"Well, the farmer had his son with him. Your grandfather looked over at the child, who was about seven years old, and asked how he was doing," Biruk said.

"Sometimes too much talk can be dangerous," Enanu whispered quietly.

"Ayat stops all the time to talk to the farmers. This has never been a problem before," responded Debritu.

"The boy your grandfather spoke to got sick this afternoon," Biruk said. "That's never happened before."

"How sick?" Debritu asked, this time a little more concerned.

"I was in town buying grain this afternoon when the boy's father came looking for the doctor. Later, I saw the father come out of the doctor's house. He was screaming for revenge," Biruk said.

"What did the doctor say?" Debritu asked.

"Apparently, the doctor told him to come back when he had some money. This embarrassed the farmer in front of his friends," Enanu said.

Debritu knew that the doctor wouldn't help the boy unless he was paid, and none of the local farmers had that kind of money. But Debritu's grandfather did.

"Maybe the strangers are here to ask for money to pay for the doctor," Debritu offered.

"I'm sure they're not here to drink coffee with Falasha potters and weavers," Enanu said bitterly.

"This could change everything," Debritu overheard her aunt say to Biruk.

Debritu thought about the farmers and villagers who lived around them. She knew they believed that the Falashas were *budas*, evil spirits who could cast spells. The children of the Beyta Israel rarely mingled with the others outside of school. When Debritu and her friends went out to fetch water for the night, they tried to avoid the group of boys from the nearby village who were out in the fields collecting twigs for their fires. Debritu remembered how one day, before they could get to the well, Gevere, the school bully, jumped out at the girls from behind a cluster of eucalyptus trees. He put down the bundle of branches that were tied to his back and began to taunt them.

"Falasha women cover themselves in the ashes left from their fires after they finish burning their clay into pots," Gevere yelled out to them. A group of his friends gathered around him. "They roll and roll, until they turn into hyenas. The ashes turn into tails and then they roam around looking for other peoples' children to eat," Gevere called out to Debritu as she passed with her friends.

"Stop talking nonsense," Debritu yelled back. Debritu, who was a little bigger than most of her friends, knew they depended on her to defend them against the bullies.

"You're a liar," Debritu called out. When Gevere stuck his tongue out at her, she couldn't stand it any more. She ran toward Gevere, pummeling him several times before they both fell to the ground. Debritu kept on hitting the boy, pulling at his tattered clothes, even though she could feel Gevere smacking away at her own face. Before her friends managed to pull her away, Debritu had a black eye and scratches down her cheek. But she was proud that she had managed to give Gevere a bloody nose.

Chapter Nine
DANGER

IT WAS ALREADY DARK WHEN DEBRITU ran back to her grandparents' home. From a distance, she could see two angry men coming out of the house, shaking their fists.

"You will be sorry," the larger man said. "Our brother is only asking for two cows and five chickens. It is a small price to pay for making his son sick."

"But the boy is better. I went into town and paid for the doctor. He's been to see the child. You told me yourself that the boy is well now," Debritu's grandfather replied.

"Yes, but our brother wants to be paid for his troubles and for his embarrassment. If you don't give him the animals, he will expect something else in return," the smaller man said, angrily.

"That is not right," Ayat answered.

"We understand that you have a young boy that lives with you. Surely you would not want the boy to fall sick like our brother's son, would you?" the big man asked.

"Are you threatening me?" Ayat asked angrily.

"It would be a shame if anything were to happen to any of the grandchildren," Debritu's grandmother said quietly, standing by his side. "Maybe we should give the man the cows and chickens."

"Never," Debritu's grandfather said. "I will not pay for this nonsense, because, if I do, it will never end." Ayat stomped back into his house, slamming the door behind him.

Debritu watched the two men jump on their horses and ride off angrily, back towards the town of Gedebye. Only when they were out of the village and on the main road did Debritu step out from behind the eucalyptus trees that grew near their home.

"Your grandfather is very stubborn," Imita said, as soon as she saw Debritu.

"What do you mean?" Debritu asked.

"The man wants your grandfather's animals so that he will not look silly in front of his friends. He has lost face because Ayat paid for a town doctor that he, a poor farmer, could not afford," Imita answered.

"But surely the boy wasn't sick because of Ayat," Debritu said.

"You and I know that. But those men believe that we have an evil eye that can cast spells," Imita said.

"So why did Ayat pay for the doctor?" Debritu asked.

"Well, the boy did fall sick, and Ayat decided to pay

for the doctor to avoid trouble. Now the boy is well. Those men don't understand that your grandfather will never pay them more," Imita said.

"What will those men do, if they don't get paid?" Debritu asked.

"I'm not sure," Imita said. "But I am worried."

"Ayat will probably pay off the soldiers to keep them away," Debritu said reassuringly, but she too began to worry.

"I don't know," Imita said. "Until now, Ayat has helped to keep peace in the village and kept problems away from here. Who knows what will happen if those farmers make trouble, now that times are so hard?"

Debritu and her grandmother sat quietly, lost in their own thoughts. They could hear the croaking of the frogs and the rustling of the leaves in the trees.

"I heard that some of the villagers are planning to leave Dero-woha and travel to Jerusalem," Debritu said after some time had passed. "We could all go with them."

"How do you know about this?" asked Imita frowning.

"There is talk in the market about people leaving Ethiopia. I know that some of my friends and their families left for Jerusalem just before the rains began. Why don't we go with the next group?" Debritu asked, a bit more boldly. "Many have made the journey. We could all go together."

"I have also heard that many have died on the way,"

Imita sighed. "And I am too old to walk to Jerusalem."

"I don't think they walk all the way," Debritu said, becoming more excited. "I've heard that they walk as far as Sudan, where they are met by people from Jerusalem who help them the rest of the way."

"Your grandfather would never agree to leave," said Imita. "He says that we must wait here, until the people from Jerusalem come and get us."

"There is danger if we go and danger if we stay," Debritu said. "I would prefer to get away from here if there is trouble."

"I know, child. But right now you must get ready for bed," Imita said, pointing to the dark clouds that had begun to cover the hills.

"The rain will soon be here," she said, softly. Then, the old woman stood up, hugged her granddaughter, and kissed her on each cheek. "We will talk in the morning."

Debritu's two younger brothers were already asleep, curled underneath their woven blankets. She tucked each brother in and then got into her own straw bed on the dusty floor. Now she was alone with no one to talk to. As the rain pounded against their thatched roof, Debritu wondered what Jerusalem would be like. Even though she wanted to go, she got a sick feeling in her stomach when she thought about leaving her mother. Recently, Biruk had come back from Addis Ababa, where he had visited

133

Emama. "She is getting better slowly," Biruk had told Debritu. "It is just a matter of time before she comes home."

"You know that as soon as she can, she will come home," her grandmother had told her. But Debritu knew that her mother wasn't really in control of when she would get well. As strong as her mother was, the illness was stronger and the doctors in Addis Ababa were helping her fight it. How could Debritu possibly leave her mother behind?

And then she thought about Jerusalem and everything she had heard, ever since she was a little girl, about that wonderful city. *What would a place full of Beyta Israel be like?* she wondered, as she fell fast asleep.

* * *

Chapter Ten
THE FARENJE

DEBRITU WASN'T SURE WHAT STARTLED HER in the middle of the night. She sensed there was movement in the village, even though it was still that strange time of night, just before dawn, when the trilling of crickets had stopped but the sounds of the morning birds hadn't yet begun. She got up quietly, so as not to wake her brothers, wrapped her shawl around her shoulders, and crept over to the door of the *gojjo* to look out into the village.

Through the fog, Debritu could see a truck parked on the main road. *What was going on? Who could be visiting in the middle of the night?* Debritu wondered.

As Debritu walked through the village towards the truck, she noticed a fire burning in the distance in her uncle's *gojjo*. Whoever came in the truck must have gone to see Biruk. The girl made her way to her uncle's home and stood outside so that she could hear the discussion inside.

"We will wait for you in the Sudan," a stranger's voice could be heard.

"How will we find our way?" Biruk asked.

"Once you arrive in Khartoum, you must find the blue door in Laneway 18, in the center of town. When you knock on the door, tell them that you are on your way to your cousin's wedding. That will be the signal that you are part of our group," the stranger answered.

"How will we get to Khartoum?" Biruk asked.

"That will be up to you," the stranger replied. "You must find your own guides to help you through the mountains of Ethiopia and the desert of the Sudan. There will be people along the way who will try to help you, but I can't promise that we will be able to do very much until you get to the camps in Sudan."

And then the stranger recited a blessing in *Ge'ez*, the language that Debritu had only heard in the house of prayer when the priests blessed the people.

This stranger must be a Beyta Israel, like us, Debritu thought.

As the voices got closer to the door, Debritu crept behind the nearby sycamore tree so that she could see the stranger who would be waiting for Biruk in Khartoum.

"*Shalom*, my friend," the stranger said warmly, hugging Biruk as they came out of the *gojjo*. "And good luck on your long journey."

Debritu could barely believe her eyes as she watched the man make his way towards his truck. The stranger was a *farenje*, a white man. Debritu had never before seen a Beyta Israel with white skin.

* * *

Chapter Eleven
THE SECRET PLAN

DURING THE NEXT FEW DAYS, Debritu saw government officials visiting Ayat. Although she couldn't hear what they were saying, she could see that Imita was getting more worried with each visit. A week had gone by since the farmers had come to Dero-woha and things just seemed to be getting worse. Then, early one morning, Imita came to wake her.

"You must leave with your two brothers as quickly as possible," Imita whispered.

"What do you mean?" Debritu asked, not sure whether she was dreaming.

"The soldiers will come before the end of this week to look for your brother Ferdu," Imita said.

"How do you know?" Debritu asked, now fully awake.

"Men from the capital have sent word to Ayat that the army is coming for more soldiers. Ferdu's name is on their list. Your brother is in danger," Imita said. "You must leave with him tomorrow."

Debritu remembered the night her father had disappeared when the army had raided their village four years ago. They hadn't heard from him since, and didn't even know if he was still alive. She now feared for Ferdu.

"Is it because grandfather wouldn't pay those men?" Debritu asked.

"We'll never understand the army," her grandmother said. By the way her grandmother looked away, Debritu knew that it had something to do with those men with the knives.

"Where can we go?" Debritu asked. "And what about Emama? How will she find us?"

"Biruk was planning to leave for Jerusalem next week, but last night he met with people who will help him leave earlier. They have managed to rearrange things so that he can leave tomorrow morning. He is going with a small group from the village. It is a dangerous journey, but you will go with our people and they will watch over you."

Debritu now began to understand what the white *farenje* who had met with her uncle was talking about. Imita explained that Debritu could join one of many groups that were making their way through the mountains into Sudan. The *farenje* was from Jerusalem and he would wait for them in Sudanese refugee camps and secret meeting centers in Khartoum. Once the Ethiopian Jews arrived in Khartoum, they would be escorted to airplanes that would take them to Israel. The trip was especially difficult because the Ethiopian and Sudanese governments weren't on friendly terms with the government in Jerusalem.

"Will Biruk agree to take us with him?" Debritu asked.

"I spoke to him earlier this morning. I have convinced him to take you and your brothers," Imita said.

"But how can I leave without Emama? She might be coming home any day now," Debritu cried. It was all too sudden for her to grasp.

The old woman came over to the girl and sat down beside her. As she held Debritu in her arms, Debritu could feel her grandmother's tears. She talked to Debritu gently.

"Debritu, you must leave with your uncle. It is the only way to save your brother. You have one day to pack your things and get your brothers ready for the trip." Her grandmother went on, "I know I am asking a lot from you. You must look after your brothers as if you were their mother. You must believe me when I tell you that I love your mother. I promise to look after her when she comes home and I will make sure that she finds you."

"Does Ayat know we are leaving?" Debritu asked.

"No. He still believes that he will be able to prevent the army from taking Ferdu. And he insists that the journey to Jerusalem is too dangerous. Ayat says that, if we wait patiently, we will all be able to leave together when the time is right. But time has run out for Ferdu. You must go without saying goodbye to your grandfather," Imita explained.

"I can't even say goodbye?" asked Debritu, feeling tears come to her eyes. Even though she had wanted to go to Jerusalem, Debritu didn't want to leave like this.

"No, now you must get ready for your journey," Imita said as she got up and turned to walk out the door. "I have to make arrangements with your uncle."

Debritu looked at her brothers asleep in their beds. Ferdu was barely thirteen and Asefa was four years old. Ferdu was strong, but Debritu knew what happened to boys that disappeared into the army. He would never survive.

Yet, could they survive a long journey in the Sudanese desert? As she packed up their things into little bundles, Debritu wondered if she was really brave enough to make this journey and look after her brothers. And then she remembered her promise to her mother. Whatever happened, she would be strong for her brothers.

She woke them up gently and began to explain what had happened.

"I won't go!" Ferdu yelled at his sister. Before Debritu could say another word, Ferdu ran out of their hut towards the fields. Debritu wanted to run after him, but Asefa ran to his sister, wrapped his arms around her neck and buried his head in her shoulder.

After she finished comforting him, Debritu lifted Asefa up and put him down in the courtyard to play. There was so much to do. Debritu organized their belongings into piles. There really wasn't much. A few shirts and pants for Ferdu and Asefa, an extra dress and shawl for herself. They would each wear their only pair of shoes.

Then Debritu went to the back of the hut where she had hidden some money from her market days. Her Imita had told her that she could keep one *birr* to spend on herself. Every week, instead of buying sweets, Debritu took the *birr* and hid it in a hole she had dug in the back of their *gojjo*. When she found the money, she put it in a pouch, which she sewed to a belt. She tied the belt around her waist, under her dress.

After she finished her work, Debritu went out to get Asefa and tied him onto her back in a shawl. *It won't be long before Asefa will be too big for carrying around on my back,* she thought. *Maybe another year or two. Hopefully, by then, we'll be settled in Jerusalem.* Now, there was someone she needed to see before she left.

It was mid-morning when Debritu made her way down the muddy path to Alemitu's house with Asefa on her back. By now the housework would be finished and Debritu figured that Alemitu was probably working outside, getting her pots ready for next week's market.

Very few Beyta Israel still took their goods to Gedebye, since the government had changed the market day from Wednesday to Saturday. Saturday was the Sabbath and most Beyta Israel were in the house of prayer with their elders on this day. But because she was so poor, Alemitu continued to sell her pots and pans on market day in order to make some money.

Debritu watched as Alemitu slowly took black clay out of one pot and combined it in a bowl with the red clay and brick dust she had dug out of the hillside. The young woman's hands skillfully transformed the mixture into shapes on her wheel, as her feet pedaled to make the wheel spin. Debritu was always amazed at how the clumps of clay would slowly turn into pots for cold water and pans for hot food.

Alemitu had already finished three pans and laid them on the rocks, like lazy lizards, to soak up the sun. After they were dry, Alemitu baked them in an oven her husband had built in the corner of their *gojjo,* so that their skins would harden. No wonder Alemitu's clay pots and pans were the best in the market.

Debritu waited until Alemitu was finished before she sat down on the stool next to her and put Asefa down to play. "Time for coffee," Alemitu said as she scooped out some green coffee beans from the straw basket near the fire and put them in a pan. She fanned up the incense and spread out the grass in the traditional way. While the beans blackened, the sweet smell filled the air. She waved the rising smoke towards her as was the custom in Ethiopia. When the beans were ready, Alemitu put them into a pot of water to boil into coffee and she slowly added sugar.

"I am leaving soon," Debritu said, while Alemitu made the coffee.

"I have heard rumors," Alemitu said. Nothing was a secret in their small village.

"You could come too," Debritu said.

"How?" Alemitu said. "How would I pay my way?"

All of a sudden, Debritu realized that it would be impossible for Alemitu to join her. This was a journey she would have to make with her brothers alone. In many ways, Debritu and Alemitu were like sisters and she would miss her friend terribly. Everything Debritu knew and loved was in this village. How could she leave?

But Debritu also knew that she had no choice. Ferdu's life was in danger.

"We will see each other again someday. After all, we're best friends," Alemitu said quietly. For the first time since she realized she would have to leave her village, Debritu began to cry.

* * *

Chapter Twelve
BABYLON

FROM ALEMITU'S HOME, Debritu walked in the direction of the fields where the boys were busy watching the cattle and sheep. She knew exactly where to find Ferdu because she had followed him many times to his hiding spot, whenever he ran away from their *gojjo*.

"Go away," Ferdu said, when he saw his sister with Asefa on her back.

Ferdu was on his back in the fields, looking up at the sky. Debritu knew that the past few years had been hard for Ferdu since they had been without either parent. He wasn't old enough to take responsibility for his own life. Yet, he was too old to be taking orders from his big sister.

Debritu sat down next to him. She could feel Asefa falling asleep on her back. For a long time, the two older siblings sat next to each other without saying a word, listening to Asefa's gentle breathing.

"We have no choice but to leave. The army will come looking for you tomorrow," Debritu finally said to her brother.

"Maybe I will find our father in the army," Ferdu said angrily.

"You know that isn't possible," Debritu said. "If Abbat were still alive, Ayat would have found him by now."

"Who will take care of us and how can we leave without Emama?" said Ferdu, looking directly at his sister, with a quiet panic in his eyes. It made Debritu think of the scared little lambs she sometimes found in the hills when they strayed from their flocks.

"Ferdu, Imita has promised that when Emama gets better, she will follow us to Jerusalem. We have to believe her."

"Do you believe her?" Ferdu asked anxiously.

"Yes, I believe her. I believe that when Emama is well enough she will join us along the way. If not, she will meet us in Jerusalem," Debritu said. "Besides, I need you, Ferdu. And Asefa needs you. Our small family must stay together."

The two sat quietly again for awhile, with Asefa asleep on Debritu's back. Then Debritu began to tell Ferdu a story she had been told by their uncle.

"Remember the story Biruk once told us about the Israelites in Babylon?" she asked her brother. "A very long time ago, the people of Israel were very sad because a terrible war had destroyed their Temple in Jerusalem,"

Debritu began. "A bad king conquered the land of Israel and sent all the Jews to Babylon, vowing that they would never live in Jerusalem again. But time passed and the Israelites grew strong and brave. They decided to go home to Jerusalem as a people, where they could live together in freedom. Slowly the people returned from Babylon and rebuilt their home."

"Where is Babylon?" Ferdu asked.

"Biruk said that, at that time, Babylon was in a place people now call Iraq. But today, Babylon is any place where people aren't free to live equally," Debritu responded.

"Like the Jews in Ethiopia," Ferdu said, suddenly understanding what his sister was trying to tell him.

"Exactly," Debritu answered. "The journey to freedom is always hard and we must be brave. Now let's go back and gather our things. It is time to prepare for our departure."

* * *

Chapter Thirteen
THE EMERALD

"THERE IS NEWS FROM ADDIS ABABA. Your mother is better and soon she will be told about your journey," Imita told Debritu, after she returned from the field with her brothers. "Go safely and she will join you in Jerusalem." The old woman who would remain at home and the young girl who was going on a long journey hugged each other tightly.

"There is one more thing," said Imita as she pulled out something that had been tucked into the sleeve of her dress.

Debritu's grandmother unwrapped a small, yellow, wrinkled and frayed cotton cloth that had some writing on it. A beautiful green stone was inside. It shimmered and glowed as if it had a life of its own. Debritu stood silently for a moment, gazing at the emerald.

"It's the emerald from the legend Emama told me about. But where did you get it?" Debritu finally asked.

"This stone was given to me by my mother," Imita said. "And her mother gave it to her. When my mother gave it to me she said that it was very old, older than we can ever imagine. She said that it came from the Ark of the Covenant in the Temple in Jerusalem. And now I'm giving it to you, my granddaughter."

"What should I do with it?" Debritu asked.

"You must pass it on to where it belongs," Imita answered cryptically.

"What do you mean?" Debritu asked.

"The writing on the cloth will tell you what to do. Until now no one has been able to read what it says. But maybe, one day in Jerusalem, you will learn what it means," her grandmother answered.

"So the stories of the Ark are real," Debritus said, astonished. "But, Imita, why are you giving me the emerald?"

"I am giving it to you to take on your journey, because I know it will keep you safe, and you will return it to where it belongs," Imita replied.

Debritu took the emerald in her palm and stared at it for a few more minutes. The stone felt warm in her hand and slowly her fingers began to tingle. Then she felt the warmth in her arms and shoulders, as a steady flow of heat passed from the emerald to the rest of her body. The emerald seemed to hold a secret.

* * *

Part Three

The Long Journey

En Route to Jerusalem
August to November, 1984

Chapter One
SAYING GOODBYE

T HE CHILDREN WOULD HAVE TO LEAVE the village without saying goodbye to their grandfather. Imita had sent Ayat to Gedebye to buy supplies for the Sabbath, knowing that he would be eager to go into town to hear the latest news, and wouldn't be back until the next morning. There was no time left to convince Ayat that leaving the village for Jerusalem was the best choice for the children. He would understand when the army came looking for his grandson.

When it came time for their departure, Debritu hugged her grandmother tightly one last time, wiping the stinging tears from her eyes. Her grandmother held her for a long time before she kissed her gently on both cheeks. Then she handed Debritu a satchel with food packets she had lovingly made for the journey. "These should last you for several weeks," Imita said as she stroked Debritu's hair.

Debritu wondered whether she would ever see Imita again. She was leaving Dero-woha, the only home she had ever known. Slowly, she turned towards her brothers waiting next to the mule that was piled with their few belongings. The three children were solemn as they got their things ready. Debritu was afraid that if she tried to speak she would begin to cry. The last thing she wanted was for the boys to see just how sad and frightened she really was. She had to be brave for their sake.

The sun was beginning to set and now they would need to hurry to meet the rest of the travelers, who were waiting for them on the outskirts of town. As they tied one last bundle of food to the side of their mule, Debritu decided to tell Ferdu what their grandmother had said about their mother. The story of the emerald she kept to herself. Finally, the three children and the mule walked away from the village, looking back on their grandmother and Dero-woha for the very last time. As she faced forwards, Debritu saw Ferdu wipe his eyes with his sleeve.

When the children reached the group, the sun had already set into the hills. A strange quiet fell upon the nervous pilgrims who surrounded Debritu's uncle, their leader in this journey, as he described what was ahead of them. "Most of our walking will be done during the night, so that we won't be seen," Biruk explained to them. "For the next few weeks, daytime will be the time for sleeping and resting." After Biruk introduced the group to their two guides, they set out on their journey. They would have to trust their guides for everything, Biruk told them, pointing at two burly men who carried guns in their belts.

With Asefa on her back, Debritu and Ferdu walked at the front of the group. Full gourds of water and baskets of food swayed from the sides of their mule. Debritu thought about Queen Yehudit hiding from her enemies in these same Ethiopian hills. Debritu would try to be as brave as Yehudit. When she looked at Ferdu, Debritu could tell that he was scared. Deep inside, the 14-year-old girl was also afraid. But she would try her best to hide it from her brothers.

That first night they walked up and down the Ethiopian hills. In the background, they could hear the distant howling of hyenas and the sharp barks of jackals. Sometimes, they caught sight of bats flying by against the backdrop of the starlit sky. When they tried to speak to each other, the children were told to be quiet. Loud voices might attract wild animals, or even worse, Ethiopian army soldiers who would send them back. With each footstep, Debritu tried to sink her worries into the ground until, finally, the familiar chirps of morning birds and the rustling of monkeys in the acacia trees reminded her that they would soon stop to rest. When Biruk and his guides found a spot in the bush close to the river, he sent the order for everyone to stop. Here they could replenish their water and rest until nightfall.

"Stay close to the trees," Biruk reminded them, as they unpacked their few things. The children were exhausted. Debritu took the water gourds and gave her brothers some to drink. Then she splashed their faces so that they would be alert enough to eat properly. There were other children in the group, but as far as Debritu could tell, they were the only ones there without their parents. They would need their strength to keep up.

"Tell us a story," Ferdu requested, as the little family settled into their first stop on the road. Debritu was happy to oblige, but first she carefully divided up a food packet of dried banana and beans between the three of them. She had to make the food last as long as possible, since Biruk had estimated it would take them close to four weeks to get to the Sudanese border.

"First finish eating," Debritu said to her brothers, relieved that after their first night of walking, Ferdu was too famished and exhausted to really worry about what was ahead of them. It didn't take long to finish their meals and put up their tents. Once they were settled, the children relaxed and Debritu began to tell them the story of the hare and the hippopotamus.

"Hare was considered the slyest animal in the forest," Debritu began. "And no one trusted him. One day, Hare decided to go out and trick Hippo. Hare asked Hippo if he could try to pull him out of the lake.

"'What will I get if you can pull me out of the lake?' asked Hippo, thinking that Hare would never be able to pull him out.

"'You can eat me for your dinner,' Hare replied.

"Hippo agreed and Hare quickly tied a rope around Hippo's tail. Then Hare went to the elephant that was eating nearby. Hare asked if he could try to pull the elephant into the lake.

"'What will I get if you can pull me into the lake?' Elephant asked.

"'You can eat me for your dinner,' Hare responded.

"'Fine,' said Elephant.

"So Hare tied the other end of the rope to Elephant's tail. Then Hare went to the middle of the rope and gave it a big tug. The elephant and the hippopotamus each started to pull on the rope. They pulled and pulled, back and forth, in and out of the lake. Finally, they both fell down exhausted in the middle of the forest. Then they saw that they each had ropes tied around their tails.

"'I am going to kill that hare!' they both exclaimed.

"In the meantime, Hare skipped home happily, because his vegetable patch was between the lake and the forest. Now, it had all been turned over, thanks to the elephant and the hippopotamus. Hare could plant his seeds without having to do any work himself."

From the sound of the breathing around her, Debritu

could tell that her listeners had fallen asleep. *I'll probably have to tell the end of my story again tomorrow,* Debritu thought. Their first night of walking in the mountains had come to an end.

* * *

Chapter Two
SHIFTAS

WITH HER BROTHERS ASLEEP DEBRITU decided to go find Biruk and tell him what Imita had said about her mother joining them in Jerusalem. Maybe he knew something about Emama as well. She checked on her brothers to make sure they were comfortable, then she walked past the weary travelers who were getting ready to rest along the edges of their camp.

The sun had just risen over the treetops when Debritu heard the sound of voices coming from the direction of the trees. She quietly walked towards them. Suddenly, Debritu stopped and took a step backwards. The voices weren't speaking in Amharic.

These people aren't from our group, she thought with alarm. Debritu hid behind a tree, from where she could see more clearly. From the way they were dressed, she could tell the men she saw weren't Ethiopians. A closer look and Debritu could see their two guides talking to two strangers who also carried rifles. While the four men gestured wildly to each other, speaking a language she didn't understand, Debritu held her breath. Then the four men split up. She watched while the two guides ran towards the hills and the other two walked towards the group.

Suddenly, Debritu understood what was happening. These men were here to rob them. *We are in trouble,* Debritu thought, as the extent of the danger began to sink in. But there was no time to let fear overcome her or warn anyone. The *shiftas* were on their way to her group. Debritu quickly took off her money belt from under her dress, took out a few *birr* and put them in her pocket. Then she dug a hole under the tree where she was standing, put the money belt in it, and covered it with a big rock. By the time she ran back to where her brothers and friends were sleeping, the robbery was already underway and the robbers had multiplied.

Debritu watched while ten bandits with guns surrounded the group of sleepers. At gunpoint, the tired travelers were awakened and told to stand up. They were instructed to put their hands in the air, while several of the *shiftas* began rummaging through their belongings. Quickly, Debritu ran towards her brothers. She hoped they wouldn't hear how hard her heart was beating or see her shaking knees. When she reached Ferdu and Asefa, she said, "Don't be afraid. Just do what they say and they won't hurt you."

One of the bandits shouted for their money. With a trembling hand, Debritu reached into her pocket and gave him the few bills she had put there. Satisfied, he walked on to the next family group. Debritu watched, afraid to move, as the men went from family to family, taking money from all the bewildered travelers. *Please don't find my emerald,* Debritu prayed. *And please stay away from my brothers* . . . .

From where she stood, Debritu looked around for their guides, but they were still nowhere to be seen. When the *shiftas* had taken as much as they wanted, they left. For the next hour everyone ran around in complete confusion, checking to see just how much was taken. Fortunately, the *shiftas* never touched the shawl where she had hidden the emerald.

When the commotion had died down, Debritu left Ferdu to watch over Asefa while she returned to her tree. The rock remained untouched. She quickly dug up her money belt and tied it back onto her waist. Then she hurried back to the camp to find Biruk.

When she found her aunt and uncle, they were busy calming down the worried travelers, who were afraid that they would never make it safely out of Ethiopia. They began demanding a safer route to Sudan.

"But this is the only way," Biruk told them. After a heated argument with a worried father who was threatening to return to the village with his children, Biruk sent everyone back to their makeshift tents. They were only one day into their journey and already Biruk was looking tired.

Debritu went over to her uncle to warn him that the guides weren't trustworthy. She told him that she had seen the guides with the *shiftas* in the forest, and that they were the ones who led the bandits to the camp. She gently suggested that he should find other guides.

"Are you sure you saw our guides with the *shiftas*?" Biruk asked, frowning.

"I am positive," Debritu said.

"Now I understand," Biruk said. "I was wondering where our guides were, while we were being robbed. You are right. We will have to hire new guides."

"Do we have enough money to do that?" Debritu asked.

"We have no choice," Biruk said. "We will collect more money in the evening."

Like Debritu, almost everyone had managed to hide away some money before settling in for their sleep. Biruk's group was quickly learning the skills they needed to survive while away from home.

Debritu walked quietly back to her little family in the bush. From a distance she could see that Ferdu was sitting up, wide awake. She straightened her shoulders and held her head high so Ferdu wouldn't suspect that she was worried. Fortunately, Asefa was sound asleep.

"We are still not too far from home. We can always go back tonight," Ferdu said when he saw his sister.

"No, there is no need," Debritu said, trying to sound convincing. "Besides, there is only danger at home. We will continue."

"But this journey is too dangerous," Ferdu argued. "When the sun sets tonight, there will be a group heading back to the village. Maybe we should go back with them."

"No, Ferdu, there is nothing for us in our village but hunger and fear," Debritu said to her brother, trying hard not to cry. "We can't go back. We must go on."

* * *

Chapter Three
CROSSING THE HIGHLANDS

S LOWLY DEBRITU AND HER BROTHERS became accustomed to traveling each night, keeping their eyes open for wild animals and *shiftas*. As they walked through the highlands, Debritu worried about nighttime leopards coming too close but relaxed when the ibex began to peek out at them from between the eucalyptus trees at dawn. As they got closer to Sudan, the soft red earth, that the Ethiopians from the Gondar area knew so well, began to turn into hard, rugged, grey rock beneath their feet and the walking became more difficult.

When it became impossible to find grasslands in which to sleep, Biruk's group got used to sleeping under the open stars, huddled together for safety. Sometimes their little group would rest where other groups were also stopped. Ferdu and Debritu would then ask around to see if anyone had seen their mother. From the strangers, Debritu learned that a terrible famine was spreading over Ethiopia.

Now Debritu began to understand how hard her

grandfather had worked to keep the famine away from the families in Dero-woha. Over the past few years, Ethiopia, a country prone to drought and famine, had suffered even more because of harsh government policies. Mengistu, Ethiopia's dictator, had been moving farmers from their villages to government-run farming communes, leaving many families with no one to work their own land. It was only because of Ayat and his bribes that the soldiers allowed his extended family to continue working in their village. The others around them were starving and were leaving their highland homes to look for food.

"There is food in the camps in Sudan," a stranger told her. "It is our only hope."

Occasionally, someone would say they had seen a woman who matched the description of their mother. But it always turned out to be someone else. Just as they were beginning to give up hope, the children stopped one day to talk to an old man in a tattered robe. As he stroked his long white beard, he said that he had seen a woman who might be their mother. The children sipped their water and listened carefully to his story.

"We stopped to rest at a camp two days ago," the old man said. He spoke very quietly and the children could see he was weak. Debritu wondered how the old man would ever finish his journey to Sudan. "She walked from person to person, asking everyone if they had seen three children – one girl and two boys," the man said.

"Was she alone? Were any family members traveling with her?" Debritu asked, as she looked into his tired eyes.

"As far as I could tell, there were no family members with her," the old man answered.

"Where was she headed?" Ferdu asked.

"She was headed towards Jerusalem," the old man said.

"Where did she come from?" Ferdu asked.

"The woman said she was coming from Addis Ababa and that her children had joined a group that began its journey from a village named Dero-woha, just outside of Gedebye. She was looking for them and hoping she would find them," he said.

At this point, Ferdu and Debritu looked at each other and for the first time in a very long while, they smiled at each other. They could barely contain their excitement as the questions poured out of them. Was it possible to believe that their mother was close by?

"Did she stay longer or did she continue with the group?" Debritu asked.

"When was the last time you saw her?" Ferdu asked.

"I don't know, children," the man said gently. "Is she your mother?" he asked.

"Our mother set out from Addis Ababa," Debritu said. "She is looking for us and we're looking for her."

"She is very close," he said, looking straight at Debritu.

"Thank you, old friend," Debritu said, as she reached into her pocket and pulled out some stale bread still left from her grandmother's packets. She gently put the food in the old man's hand and walked away.

The sun was beginning to set and Debritu knew that soon the guides would send word for the group to begin another long night of walking. It had been weeks since they had set out with their new guides and Debritu watched as her brothers grew thinner and weaker. Every day as she packed up their blankets, rolled up their few belongings and tied them to the side of the mule she worried about their shrinking provisions. The spreading famine meant that food in the area was becoming more scarce and expensive. Since the *shiftas* had robbed them, the group had been left with less money to buy food along the way. Everyone was beginning to wonder just how long they could go with so little to eat.

For a moment, Debritu wondered whether she had made a mistake giving the old man the bread. But surely they would be able to manage with what they had until they got help. She wasn't sure that the old man could last without food for too much longer. For comfort, Debritu took out the emerald and held it in her hand to feel its warmth. *Where did you come from?* Debritu wondered. And somehow the emerald gave her the strength to keep on going.

"Come on, Asefa," Debritu said as she picked up her brother and put him on the mule. Over the past day or so, Asefa had stopped speaking. No matter how much Debritu tried to coax him, he wouldn't say a word.

The small rations of bread and sips of water just aren't enough for my brothers, she thought. She was beginning to see the shape of their bones through their skin, and as hard as she tried, she couldn't stop worrying. Debritu began to wonder if Ferdu had been right about returning to Derowoha. But there was no turning back at this point. They would have to go on.

Reluctantly, Debritu and Ferdu set out for one more night of marching through the desert. They walked for half the night in single file. At last, word spread through the group that they had arrived at the Sudanese border.

"Stay here with the rest of the group," Biruk told his niece. "I am going to speak to the Sudanese soldiers. Our only hope for food and water is to get to the other side."

"Emama is near," Debritu told her uncle and explained to him what the old man had said.

"I'll look out for her," he answered, as he walked off with the guides towards a police station in the distance. Debritu could see hundreds of people in tattered clothes already waiting outside the station. They all wanted to be allowed into Sudan.

"Good luck," Debritu yelled out to her uncle.

Chapter Four
THE REBELS

WE CAN'T GO ON LIKE THIS, Debritu thought, as she tossed and turned underneath her blanket. It had been a while since they had eaten anything more than one dry piece of bread each day. She was too hungry and worried to sleep. Debritu looked at her sleeping brothers and wondered how she could keep them safe for much longer. Like a desert storm, danger seemed to be closing in on them from every direction.

The stars were all gone but the sun hadn't quite pierced through the morning sky. Debritu decided to get up and see what she could find for them to eat. The earth had become drier and harder. And trees were becoming few and far between. *Maybe I'll come across a lone desert berry on an overlooked bush or an animal that I can trap,* she thought. At the very least, she might be able to find some shrubs to chew on.

She hadn't gotten too far before someone yelled at her, "Stop, or I'll shoot!"

"Who are you?" Debritu asked, not seeing anyone.

"I'm the one with the gun, so I'm the one who gets to ask the questions," a young male voice replied.

"I'm just a girl looking for food," Debritu said. Her heart was pounding so hard, she could feel it in her empty stomach.

"Where are you from?" the voice asked.

"From a small village near Gedebye," Debritu said, as she tried to figure out where the voice was coming from.

"Where are you going?" the voice demanded.

"We left our village in search of food," Debritu replied, afraid to tell the stranger any more.

"By yourself?" the voice asked.

"I am with my brothers," Debritu said, "And we are very hungry. I left them asleep so that I could look for food."

"Come with me," the voice ordered, as he came out from the bushes, pointing a rifle at her.

"You are barely older than me," Debritu said.

"And you are barely younger than me," the boy said gruffly, as he marched her deeper into the darkness. Within a few minutes, she was in a campsite where other boys and girls were sleeping around a smoldering fire.

"Get up everyone. I have a visitor," the boy said. "And she's looking for food."

"Who are you?" Debritu asked the small group of about a dozen boys and girls, who were slowly getting up to look at Debritu. They were dressed in torn shirts and ragged pants, but they all seemed to have guns at their sides.

"We're soldiers fighting this corrupt government," one of the girls said, as they inspected the new visitor.

"Who are you?" another girl asked.

"My name is Debritu. I left my home near Gedebye to look for food," Debritu said.

"Join us," another girl said. "We need more soldiers to help us because the army keeps getting bigger all the time. But don't worry, they'll never beat us."

"I can't join you," Debritu said, cautiously. "I have my brothers to look after. One is twelve, but the other is only four. And they're so weak, they can barely walk. Besides," she added, "How will fighting help? Will fighting bring us more food?"

"We want a new leader for Ethiopia. We need a leader who will use this country's money to feed his people, not to buy tanks and airplanes," a boy shouted.

"We need a leader who won't steal boys and men away from their families to fill his army," said another boy.

For a few minutes, Debritu was quiet. She remembered how people in her village spoke about the rebels and how dangerous they were. Aside from the boy with the gun who had brought her to the campsite, the rest of the group didn't seem dangerous. Could she trust the rest of them? They were inviting her to join them. She thought about her own father who had been taken away from his family. Maybe some of the things the rebels were saying made sense. But she certainly didn't want to run away from one army, just to join another. Anyhow, she had promised her mother that she would keep her family safe.

"I can't stay. I need to get back to my brothers with some food or they'll die," Debritu said, when she had finally made her decision.

"So you won't join us?" the boy with the gun questioned her sternly.

"No, I need to help my brothers. My brothers will die, if I don't help them," Debritu said, getting ready to go.

"Let's make her stay," said the angry boy to the others. "She has no right to leave without helping her people."

"Don't be silly," a girl said, shooting a disapproving look at the boy. Then she turned to Debritu and said, "He is tired and foolish from living in the forests. Don't worry, he won't bother you."

"Here is some food," she added, giving Debritu a basket with some boiled eggs, a few tomatoes and one very big potato.

"I'll take her back to the road," the girl said, slinging her rifle over her shoulders.

* * *

Chapter Five
BORDER OF SUDAN

"LOOK WHAT I'VE BROUGHT YOU TO EAT," Debritu said, as she woke her brothers up, showing them the food the rebels had given her. Ferdu came to sit beside her and the two of them could barely believe their good fortune. She carefully cut up one egg and one tomato, saving the rest for later.

"This is so tasty," Ferdu said as he ate hungrily. "Where did you get it?"

"I met some children in the forest," Debritu said, as she tried to coax Asefa into eating a bit of egg. Over the past few days, Asefa had lost interest in everything around him. He seemed to be getting weaker with each passing hour. Even opening his mouth seemed to be too great an effort.

"He won't eat anything," Debritu said, impatiently. "I just don't know what to do."

Before Ferdu could answer, Biruk yelled out to the group. "Pack up your belongings, we're moving on. We'll wait at the police station until they let us pass."

"When will this trip ever end?" Ferdu asked as they packed up their things for one more night of walking.

With food in her stomach, Debritu managed the walk to the police station without too much trouble. But once they arrived at the station, it became clear that it wouldn't be easy to cross the border. Now Debritu began to really worry. With Asefa so sick, it seemed as if they didn't have much time to waste.

The sun rose and set. Another day and a night passed and still Debritu and her group waited while Biruk tried to persuade the soldiers to allow them into Sudan. Debritu looked at all the people sitting around the station. They were staring blankly into space. It seemed as if they had been waiting there forever. They moved only to fan away the endless stream of flies that settled on their faces. There was something very unsettling about the look in their eyes. It was as if they had given up all hope.

Debritu understood the look of despair. It was so hot that even the smallest gestures hurt. Debritu and her brothers were so thirsty, but they were afraid to use up their water because no one knew where they would get any more. For a minute she thought about joining the people who were waiting so quietly by the police station. Then she remembered her promise to her mother. If she gave up, there would be no one to look after her brothers. She took Ferdu and Asefa and sat on the other side of the station.

All of a sudden, Debritu noticed a boy in the crowd outside the station who looked familiar. It took her a minute to figure out how she knew him. He looked different, but there was something about his eyes that reminded Debritu of home. And then it hit her. It was Gevere, the boy who had constantly teased her by calling her Falasha. It was the boy that fought with her outside her village and gave her a black eye. He was so skinny now. His arms and legs looked like the twigs they had carried home from the fields. His stomach was swollen in the way that meant Gevere had gone hungry for a very long time.

"Gevere, what are you doing here?" Debritu asked, as she approached the boy.

Gevere just looked at her blankly.

"It is me, Debritu," said Debritu. "Remember, you gave me a black eye. You called me a Falasha."

"Go away," Gevere said. "I have no food for you."

"I don't care about the black eye. Or about you calling me Falasha," Debritu said. Their differences meant very little here. Debritu thought about their home near Gedebye and felt tears come to her eyes. She missed everything about Dero-woha – Imita, Ayat, her best friend and even her chores. She wondered how her grandparents were doing and whether she would ever see them again.

"Go away," Gevere said, this time a little less forcefully.

"Here," Debritu said, handing a tomato to Gevere. He took it quickly. Debritu knew that they didn't have much food left, but Gevere looked so hungry and desperate. At least they still had a potato and some eggs.

"What are you doing here?" Debritu asked once again after Gevere had eaten the tomato. Slowly, Gevere reminded Debritu how his father had been taken away by the soldiers to work on a communal farm. They waited for him for months, but like Debritu's father, he didn't come back. Without anyone to defend their family's belongings, they had lost all their cattle to soldiers and rebels. And without rain, no crops would grow in their fields. Like many others, they could no longer feed themselves.

"We heard that there were refugee camps in Sudan with food for everyone to eat. So my family gathered whatever they could carry and began walking into the mountains towards the west," Gevere explained. "But the hills were full of *shiftas* and they stole what little we had left. And now the camps are full, and we have nowhere to go." Gevere held back his tears.

"It will get better," Debritu said. "Wait and see. They will bring more food."

Gevere and Debritu nodded to each other, but they both knew that it was unlikely that they would receive food here. The two sat silently watching the vultures and ravens gather in the empty branches of the lone trees standing on the Sudanese side of the deserted field. This earth had not grown any food for a very long time. Debritu wished she could make Gevere feel better. But she really didn't know what else to say. Finally, Debritu got up and went back to find her brothers.

"All these people are hoping that eventually they will get to one of the camps in Sudan," Ferdu said to Debritu when she found their little group.

"Will they let everyone in?" Ferdu asked. Both looked worriedly at their little brother. Asefa was lying on his side with his eyes closed.

"They say that all the refugee camps are full," Biruk said when he came out of the police station. "They want us to go back to Ethiopia," he added anxiously.

"Go back in and tell them that we can't go back. We will all die," a woman cried out. No one wanted to think about the members of their group who had already died from sickness or starvation along the way. The group, which had dwindled from over 100 to less than 50, stared at the man who had led them this far. They were the brave ones who had not gone back. They knew that, with so little food left, they would not survive if they turned back now.

"I'll try again," Biruk said. Debritu and her brothers

drew closer together and watched while Biruk went back into the police station. Debritu held her breath and wondered what would happen if the guards wouldn't let them pass the border. Finally, Biruk came out of the station with the news they were waiting for.

"Hurry up, before they change their minds," he told the group, as everyone got to their feet, ready to cross through the building that stood next to the lake that separated Ethiopia from Sudan.

Debritu put Asefa on her back. He was now as light as a feather and she wondered how much longer he could survive. Ferdu rose to his feet and put their blankets on their mule. The children walked together at the edge of the bedraggled group. Everyone seemed so tired. But there was no choice. They had to go on. At least, they were now crossing the border into Sudan.

"Is there any food for my starving people?" Biruk asked the guards when they had reached the other side of the border.

"Walk in that direction," one of the guards said gently. "They are giving out bags of rice."

They continued to walk until they saw a station in the distance with tables holding sacks of rice. Beyond the station was a lake, filled with dirty, muddy water, where other groups were already settled into makeshift camps.

"Go down to the lake and set out your things," Biruk

told the group. "And don't forget to boil the lake water before you drink it. I'll go get sacks of rice for us."

That night, with the last of the egg and potato, Debritu and Ferdu ate until their bellies felt satisfied for the first time in a long time. But Debritu could only get Asefa to eat a spoonful or two of rice before he turned away to stare into the distance.

"Will we ever make it to Jerusalem?" Ferdu asked.

"Of course, we will," Debritu answered, aware that Ferdu was beginning to give up hope. She tried to hide her own doubts from Ferdu, yet deep down inside she too was beginning to wonder if they would ever make it to Jerusalem. She had never expected the journey to be this difficult. She dreaded the beginning of each day. The only thing that kept her going was the promise she made to her mother.

"First we must find Emama," said Debritu. "Tomorrow we begin our search once again. Look around carefully. She might even be here."

They were surrounded by other groups of Ethiopians crossing the border hoping to find food for their families. Some of them planned to settle in refugee camps until the food shortage was solved in Ethiopia. Others were Ethiopian Jews, like Debritu and her brothers, making their way to Jerusalem. It was hard to tell them apart.

Debritu and Ferdu sat quietly, looking at and listening

to their fellow travelers as they settled into their blankets. By the time night fell, there was nothing to do but sleep.

Within an hour or two, the three of them were awakened by the sound of thunder as the rain began to fall. It was a flash downpour, the kind of rain that only falls in the desert.

"I am afraid," Asefa said.

"It is nothing but rain," Debritu said to her frail little brother as she held him close. It was the first time she had heard him speak in days. The three children lay near each other and shivered as the rain came down in an endless pour.

* * *

Chapter Six
THE ROAD TO DOKA

"IT IS TIME TO MOVE ON," Biruk announced suddenly. After ten days of rice and waiting, a truck came to the campsite by the lake. Earlier that morning, Biruk had come by to ask for more money from everyone in the group, explaining that he would need more to buy room on the truck that would take them to Doka, their next stop in the desert.

"I need a doctor for Asefa," Debritu said to her uncle, as she handed him money for the trip. Asefa's nose had been bleeding for several days and he could barely sit up straight.

While the group searched through their last few *birr* to see what they could collect, Debritu watched Biruk talk to three Sudanese men wearing white robes and square caps. They looked so big next to her uncle.

"How much will it cost to take this group to Doka?" she overheard her uncle ask.

"We will look for a doctor later," Biruk said as he walked back, tired and stooped. Debritu didn't know whether to believe him.

Quietly, Debritu and Ferdu packed up what little was left of their belongings. There really wasn't much to say to each other.

"The mule will stay here," Debritu told her brother, as she tied their things into a bundle and told Ferdu to carry it on his back. Debritu felt bad about leaving their mule, but they had no choice. They couldn't expect the mule to get on a truck while so many people were waiting for a spot. All they would have left was each other and a handful of belongings. It had been days since Debritu had taken the emerald out of its hiding place. What good could the emerald possibly do for her now? The last time she looked at it, she wondered whether she would be the last person to ever hold it.

She put Asefa into her shawl and tied him onto her back. She felt his head rest gently on her back. He was now so light she could barely feel his weight. His breath felt like the fluttering wings of a small butterfly. Quietly, they waited, until Biruk gave them the sign to get onto the truck. Then everyone piled onto the old and rusty truck as quickly as they could.

By the time they began to move, Debritu felt that she was drowning in a sea of hands and feet that poked at her from all directions. She cradled Asefa in her arms and then elbowed her way into an empty bit of space. With Ferdu at her side, they settled into the bumpy ride.

"I'm thirsty," Ferdu said.

"Try to wait," Debritu answered. She wasn't sure how long it would be before they would be able to fill their gourds with water again. The children rested against each other, as the truck rattled along the muddy road.

Suddenly, the truck lurched back and forth and came to a full stop. Debritu could hear the truck doors slam and the drivers arguing with each other. The heat inside the truck was unbearable. Debritu felt as if she would suffocate if she stayed inside too much longer but it didn't seem as if they were going to move in the near future. Debritu looked around at the other people. They were all beginning to squirm as the heat pressed down hard against them.

"We have to get out," Debritu said to her brother. "We'll die in here."

Slowly word went through the group that they would unload until they could figure out what was wrong. Exhausted, Debritu and her brothers got out of the truck and stood at the side of the muddy road. The previous day's rains had made the road unpassable. The truck was stuck in a hole the size of a small lake and couldn't get out. It was clear that this truck wasn't going anywhere no matter how much Biruk argued with the driver.

Finally Biruk got his money back from the drivers and told everyone that they would need to walk back a short distance. There was a herd of camels nearby and he was going to negotiate with their owner. Doka was still far and it was clear that many in the group were just too tired and weak to survive another long walk. But maybe on camels they could make it.

Debritu cried as she followed her uncle. With Asefa sick, very little food left, and no end in sight to their journey, she couldn't imagine their trip getting any worse. She forced her feet to walk, even though she just wanted to collapse down into the ground. She forced her eyes to look straight down because she couldn't bear to look at the despair on the faces around her.

I'm so tired and hungry, she thought to herself. *Maybe I could lie down for just a little while at the side of the road and catch up with the group later.*

"Don't give up," Ferdu said to her as he slipped his hand in hers. "I know we can make it." The children walked on, forcing each other to go just a bit further.

By the time Biruk found the camels and arranged for their use, it was already late in the afternoon. But Biruk insisted that they continue their journey without any further delays. With Asefa on her back, Debritu and Ferdu helped each other onto a kneeling camel. Then they put Asefa between them so that he wouldn't slip off. When everyone was finally ready, the camels stood up and turned towards the muddy road, which was even difficult for the animals to pass through.

The group moved slowly. Debritu felt as if every step pulled her aching body apart.

When she looked to the side, the sand around her looked like little fleas, ready to take her away. She closed her eyes and forced herself to hold on tight to the camel's neck as it bobbed up and down. She counted each time her camel pulled a hoof out of the deep mud, afraid that she might faint if she stopped concentrating on staying awake. Finally, towards the end of the day, they came to a campsite with tents and tables in the midst of the desert. In the distance, Debritu could see a big town.

"We get off here," Biruk instructed his group. "Eat, drink and rest. From here, we will find another truck that will take us on to Doka, and from there we will continue to Khartoum."

Sudanese guides waited with some food and water, while other camels rested at the side of the road. Other refugees walked aimlessly in circles, waiting to move on.

Debritu slid off her camel. Ferdu passed Asefa to his sister before getting off himself. Then the three children walked over to a table where a few people were standing in line for food and water. When they got to the front of the line and held out their gourds, Debritu thought she was dreaming.

The *farenje* she had seen leaving her uncle Biruk's *gojjo* in their village, the white-skinned man who spoke with her uncle, was standing behind the table, filling bowls with food.

* * *

Chapter Seven
DOCTOR IN GHADARIF

"WHO ARE YOU?" Debritu asked, as she made her way up to the front of the table. She explained that she had seen him leaving her uncle's home in Dero-woha so many weeks ago.

"I am part of a group helping the Beyta Israel find their way to Jerusalem," the man explained. He spoke Amharic with the most unusual accent Debritu had ever heard.

"Beyta Israel! That's us," Debritu announced, excited. It was the first time she wasn't called a Falasha, except by the elders who always used Beyta Israel to describe their people. Something about the way the *farenje* looked convinced her that this was a man that she could trust. He explained that many Jews from all over the world were trying to help the Beyta Israel find their way to Jerusalem.

"The journey has been very hard for us," Debritu said. "My brother is very sick. I don't know if he will make it." Then the words just poured out of Debritu's mouth. She told the man everything about their mother, their father, about their journey and about how sick Asefa was.

"You must get to Ghadarif, a large town with doctors and nurses," the *farenje* said, pointing at the town in the distance. He gave Debritu a paper with a doctor's name and a map of Ghadarif. Debritu looked at the paper with dread, knowing the choice she would have to make. To get to a doctor, they would have to leave the group. She realized that she would have to get help for her brother on her own. But how would they get to Jerusalem by themselves? How would they ever survive?

Debritu looked over at her little brother, who could hardly open his eyes, and she knew what she had to do. She would have to tell her uncle that they couldn't continue with him and the group. She and her brothers would go to Ghadarif to find a doctor for Asefa.

"We need to find help right away," Debritu said, when she found Biruk giving food out to the other people in their dwindling group. "Otherwise, Asefa will die."

"But we aren't planning to go in the direction of Ghadarif," Biruk said. "I am planning to take everyone to Doka and then to a refugee camp near Khartoum."

"I know," Debritu said, "I must find a doctor for Asefa. I will take my chances on my own with my brothers."

"If you lose your way, meet these people in Khartoum," Biruk said, sighing as he wrote some information down on a piece of paper. He was responsible for the entire group and could not change their route for one person, not even for his niece or nephews. Yet, he knew that for Asefa's sake, Debritu really had no choice. Biruk gave Debritu the piece of paper. On it was an address in Khartoum where people would be able to help her. Debritu folded up the slip of paper and put it in her belt, right next to the one the *farenje* had given her.

"Good luck and be very careful," said Biruk. He kissed Debritu on both cheeks before he turned to Ferdu and hugged him warmly. "Look after each other and remember to be brave," he said, before he turned back to his family. Debritu and Ferdu silently watched while their uncle walked back to the group. Then the three children set off on their trek towards Ghadarif.

In a few hours, Debritu, Ferdu and Asefa reached a small campsite of straw houses. Police were directing refugees to camps and towns. Debritu found a young soldier in uniform who spoke Amharic, and explained that she needed a doctor for Asefa. She showed him the piece of paper that the *farenje* had given her with the address of a doctor.

"We have family waiting for us in Khartoum," Debritu said, hoping that he would believe her. "But if I don't get a doctor for my brother now, he will die."

"A doctor will cost you money," the soldier said.

Debritu reached into her money belt and took out her last few *birr*. She prayed it was enough to pay for the doctor. The only other money she had left was just enough to get them on a bus to Khartoum. But she still had the emerald. *Maybe that's what grandmother meant,* Debritu thought. *Maybe the emerald is meant to save Asefa's life.*

"Please get us a doctor," Debritu said, as she handed over the money to the young soldier.

"I'll see what I can do. In the meantime, wait near my home," said the soldier, as he directed them to a small, mud-thatched hut at the edge of town. Debritu began to unpack their things as she watched the boy go off to the town.

While the little family waited outside the soldier's hut they used their blankets to build a makeshift roof over their heads next to the hut's wall. They ate the buns they had packed in their bags. And even though Debritu tried to force Asefa to drink little drops of water, the only thing he wanted was milk, which she didn't have.

"Should we wait for the doctor to come, or go on to Khartoum?" Debritu asked Ferdu early the next morning, when the doctor still hadn't appeared. She wanted to make the right decision for Asefa but she just didn't know what to do. She had only her brother Ferdu to ask.

"Let's wait," Ferdu said. "Without medicine, Asefa will die."

The three tired young travelers lay down under their roof made of blankets, barely moving for hours. Debritu was worried about what they would do when their food ran out, when, suddenly, a man in a white robe, speaking a strange language, came by to examine Asefa.

"He is asking for milk," Debritu told the man. But she couldn't be sure whether he understood her.

He looked inside Asefa's mouth and eyes. He listened to his heart and stomach. And then he unwrapped a handful of cream-colored pills and put them in Debritu's hand. The man lifted up one finger to show that he wanted Asefa to take one pill every day until they were finished.

"There are five pills," Debritu said staring at the pills, before she put them in her pocket. These would have to help Asefa or he would die.

"That means we'll have to stay here for at least five days until Asefa finishes his pills," Ferdu added.

"Will Asefa be well enough to continue then?" Debritu asked the doctor, but he left without answering.

"We will wait here until Asefa is well," Ferdu said with confidence. Debritu looked at her brother and held back her tears. Ferdu had grown up so much on this journey. They now depended on each other for comfort and support.

"Don't we have to pay for the medicine?" Debritu asked, wondering about the emerald.

"Apparently not," Ferdu said. "The doctor was kind. He didn't ask for money."

"Go to the police station and ask if anyone knows where we can find some food," Debritu suggested to Ferdu. "Ask if they have milk and bread."

"I want to wait here with you," Ferdu said. He seemed worried that something might happen to Asefa.

"Alright," Debritu said. "You stay here, then, and I'll go find some milk for Asefa." She would also try to find something for Ferdu to eat.

Debritu got up slowly and walked through the center of town to the police station, where a long line of people were waiting for milk mixed with cornmeal to fill their cups.

"Can I have some milk for my sick brother?" Debritu asked meekly, holding out her cup, along with everyone else.

* * *

Chapter Eight
KHARTOUM

THE FIVE DAYS PASSED SLOWLY while Asefa took his medicine. On the third day, he began to eat and drink on his own. On the fourth day, he began to ask for more food. By the fifth day, he seemed to have built up some strength and sat up for longer stretches of time. Ferdu and Debritu were finally beginning to feel hopeful that Asefa was getting better.

"When do we move on?" Ferdu asked. "Maybe we should stay here in Ghadarif."

"We will rest here for just a few more days," Debritu said. "Asefa needs to get stronger before we leave." Debritu knew that even though it was important to wait for Asefa to get better, it was getting harder to convince Ferdu to continue with their journey.

Debritu tried to insist that he stay close by, but Ferdu spent his days walking around the dusty town. He joined in the occasional game of soccer that boys his age were playing in the alleys between the ramshackle homes. Although Debritu was happy that Ferdu was strong enough to enjoy himself again, she was always relieved when her brother slipped back in at night. Finally, when Asefa began to walk around a bit, Debritu decided that he was well enough to continue the journey into Khartoum.

"Why are we going to Khartoum?" Ferdu asked.

"Because people are waiting there to take us to Jerusalem," Debritu explained.

"Why don't we just stay here?" Ferdu asked. "The people here are friendly. We can make a new home right here. Do you really believe we will ever make it to Jerusalem? I'm not even sure that Jerusalem really exists anymore."

"Ferdu, we've come this far. Trust me for just a few days longer. You'll see, Jerusalem does exist. A bus leaves for Khartoum in the morning and we're going to be on it," Debritu said. Deep inside, she herself was beginning to wonder whether they should go on to Jerusalem. It had been such a difficult journey and who knew what really was ahead of them. What if Asefa got sick again? Now they were down to their very last few *birr*.

"Do you sometimes wonder why we left our home in Ethiopia?" Ferdu asked, as he shivered slightly. The wind had begun to pick up, bringing dusty waves of sand into the air.

Debritu wrapped her shawl around her head and shoulders in a determined way. "No," she said. "I know that our lives will be better in our new home."

194

"And Emama?" Ferdu asked. "Do you think we will ever see her again?"

"I don't know," Debritu said, sighing. Since they had separated from their group, they had stopped searching for their mother. "I guess if she is alive and well, she will find us."

Debritu could barely sleep all night. Every few minutes, she got up to check on Asefa, to make sure that he was still well. From time to time, she took a peek at her emerald and at the strange writing on the paper it was wrapped in. Her grandmother's words echoed inside of her, reminding her that she had promised to keep it safe.

The next morning, Debritu sat quietly on the bus to Khartoum, looking out the window at the passing huts that dotted the hillside. When the bus finally pulled in to the Sudanese capital, Debritu stared at the teeming sea of people that surrounded them. She had never seen so many buildings, so close to each other. Hundreds of women, men and children seemed to pour out of the houses and into the streets. Everywhere she looked, she saw eyes staring at her from inside the darkness of makeshift homes, piled against the walls of crumbling buildings. She could see that Ferdu was scared, so she pulled herself up straight and tall as they continued along the dusty road.

As she came out of the bus station with Asefa on her

back, Debritu could hear the rhythmic chanting of prayers coming from a domed mosque in the center of town. Debritu looked inside at the men, kneeled down on their prayer mats.

"How will we ever find our way in this huge city?" Ferdu asked his sister, nervously. No one here spoke any language they had ever heard in Ethiopia. And they both knew that if anyone discovered they were Ethiopian, they would probably send them back.

"Don't worry. All we have to do is follow this map," Debritu said, unfolding the piece of paper Biruk had given her. Slowly, they followed the directions through the busy streets of Khartoum until they found themselves in front of a blue door on Laneway 18.

"Who is it?" someone called out in Amharic, after Debritu knocked on the door.

"We are on our way to our cousin's wedding," Debritu answered, remembering the phrase that Biruk had told her would identify them as Beyta Israel on their way to Jerusalem.

"Come in," the voice said, as a bolt was pulled from across the door.

When Debritu opened the door, she saw a handful of women inside the house, busy preparing food. Pots of stew cooked on a stove, and baskets of *injara* were placed on a table in the middle of one big room, filled with people.

Along the walls of the room were other long tables, piled with blankets, clothes and shoes.

Debritu barely finished explaining who they were when a woman in an Ethiopian dress hugged them and pulled them aside. "This is where you will stay until it is time for you to fly to Israel," she said.

Debritu and her brothers looked around at the tables filled with food and clothes. Could all this be real? Had they really reached safety? In the crowd of strange faces, Debritu noticed white *farenje* milling around. She wondered if they were from Jerusalem and if they were going to help them on the last part of their journey.

"Go take some *injara* and chicken," the woman said to the children.

"But I don't know anyone here," Debritu answered shyly.

"It is alright. We are your friends. You can take whatever we give you," the woman said.

After bringing back food for her brothers, Debritu went to choose clothes from the piles on the tables. Her dress was so tattered, it barely held together on her body. Only the shawl on her back was still intact—with the emerald safely sewn inside.

"What would you like?" asked a *farenje* woman, wearing a pair of jeans and a T-shirt. "You can have anything you want," she said with a grin.

"I'll take those runners," Debritu said, kicking off the tattered shoes she had worn all the way from Ethiopia.

* * *

Chapter Nine
ON A WING AND A PRAYER

THAT WEEK, the three children slept in the house on mats placed on the ground. Debritu and her brothers slept close together every night, afraid they would wake up and find themselves still in the Sudanese desert. Around them, they listened to the sounds of people talking in languages they had never heard before – sometimes Hebrew, other times English. And they wondered what was in the future.

"Where do you think they're taking us?" Ferdu asked his sister on the morning when they finally climbed onto a truck with other Ethiopian Jews from the house.

"Maybe they're finally taking us to Jerusalem," Debritu whispered.

The truck pulled into a large field near Khartoum where several large planes were waiting. They saw hundreds of Ethiopian Jews, waiting to be assigned a place in line before they could get on the airplanes that would take them to Jerusalem. Debritu looked at the people around her. They all looked so shockingly thin. *Am I as skinny as they are?* she wondered.

Exhausted, the men, women and children formed long lines to wait for their turns at the desk. They were all relieved to be on the last leg of their long journey but anxious about what lay ahead. As she stood in line Debritu looked at everyone, hoping to find someone familiar, but she didn't see anyone she recognized. When she got to the front of the line, a man speaking Amharic asked for their names. He wrote them down in a big book. In Israel, they would use the names to figure out who had survived the long trek from Ethiopia.

The children waited, holding hands, until a man yelled out in Amharic that it was time to board the planes for Israel.

"Ferdu, you are finally going to fly on one of those planes that split the sky," said Debritu.

"I guess you were wrong," Ferdu said happily.

"What do you mean?" Debritu asked.

"Falasha boys do fly in airplanes," Ferdu answered with a laugh.

* * *

Chapter Ten
JERUSALEM AT LAST
November 1984

WHEN DEBRITU GOT OFF THE PLANE at Lod International Airport in Israel, she found herself surrounded by people and things she had never seen before. The walls of the airport were lined with stores and restaurants. Some shops displayed boxes of chocolates and bags of candy. Others had counters filled with newspapers and books. Against another wall, there were girls in tight tank tops and low-cut jeans holding hands with boys who had long straight hair down to the middle of their backs, waiting patiently in front of ticket counters.

At the far end of the room, people sat in restaurants casually sipping hot coffee from white spongy cups and gulping down colored soda out of glass bottles.

Strange music, in a language Debritu had never heard before, was playing from speakers hanging from the ceiling. Hundreds of people milled around in the long hallway where suitcases were coming around on a black rubber belt. There were pale men with dark beards, long coats and big black hats picking up their luggage. At the far end of the

201

room, men and women in army uniforms were checking bags at the doors of the airport. Other men, wearing the kind of Arabic headscarves she had seen in Sudan, walked about waving their arms as they talked to each other.

Through the airport windows, Debritu could hear cars honking outside and taxi drivers yelling at each other to get off the road. She saw women in long embroidered dresses and headscarves, selling fruit on the curb. Large buses and trucks were unloading passengers going to and from work. All around her, people were moving about and shouting at each other and she couldn't understand a word.

Debritu and her brothers watched anxiously as the many white faces passed by in the bustle of the modern airport. There were so many people from all over the world, and they all looked so different from each other. This was not at all what Debritu had expected. Where were the Israelites she had heard so much about? Where were the Temple priests with their flowing white tunics? Where were the people who looked like her?

She held back her tears as she thought about her parents and everyone else they had left behind in Ethiopia. She remembered Dero-woha and the familiar hut where she had slept with her family, her friends who walked with her to the school and gathered at the well, her market days with Alemitu and the moonlit nights listening to Biruk's stories. Here there was no one and nothing familiar. All around her people were busy doing things she couldn't understand. Where were the people who spoke her language?

Debritu sat down on the floor, put her head down on her arms and began to cry. She had promised her mother that she would keep her brothers safe and she had succeeded. Finally able to let her guard down, she cried from exhaustion and loneliness. There was no one she could talk to and no one who could help her. How would she manage here in Israel when she couldn't speak the language or understand what anyone wanted? Without any relatives, how would she keep her little family together?

Debritu checked her pockets. She had no food and no money left. She had protected her brothers through the most difficult journey of their lives, but she didn't know if she could keep them safe any longer. The only thing she had left was her emerald.

I'm going to sell that stupid thing as soon as I can, Debritu thought to herself angrily. *I thought I would find a girl like me to return it to. Instead, this emerald has brought me to a place where no one looks or talks like me. It has brought me nothing but bad luck and I hate it.*

Still crying, Debritu looked up to check on her brothers. She almost screamed. Ferdu and Asefa were gone. How could this have happened? While she was foolishly lost in her own thoughts, they had walked away from her. Now what was she going to do?

"Asefa, Ferdu," Debritu called out as she got up and frantically began looking around. She couldn't even ask anyone for help. With so many different people doing so many strange things, Debritu felt completely helpless and lost. All of a sudden, the colors in the room began to blend with the sounds of the music and the ceiling and floor began to spin.

Do not faint, Debritu scolded herself. She had to find her brothers. In desperation Debritu moved through the crowd, looking at every face, calling their names.

There was no response. Where could they be? Debritu scanned the room again. At the far end a movement caught her eye, and she heard children squealing. Those were her brothers' voices, Debritu was sure.

Was someone hurting them? Were they yelling for her? Debritu raced toward the cries. As she came closer a strange scene unfolded before her. Yes, there were her brothers. But they were jumping up and down with excitement, not fear, and hugging someone who knelt in front of them.

Who could it be? Debritu couldn't see around her brothers. She called out to them, and as they turned to her the figure behind them stood up. Debritu's heart jumped. Were her eyes deceiving her? Was this real or just a vision?

"Mother," she whispered.

For the first time in what seemed like forever, Debritu

fell into her mother's arms. "I can't believe it's you," she sobbed, hugging her closer. The boys grabbed on to their mother and sister and the little family was wrapped tightly in each other's arms, laughing and crying as if they were in their own private world. They were together at last.

Finally, Debritu asked her mother, "How did you get here?"

"What happened to you?" Ferdu called out.

"How long have you been here?" Debritu cried out. The questions rushed out of them so quickly that Emama began to laugh.

"Children," Emama said, gathering them into her arms. "You'll have to calm down before I can answer any of your questions."

When they had settled down, Emama told them her story. She had been on the verge of recovering when she heard that her children had left their village for Jerusalem. Before that, on one of his visits, Biruk had told her that a group of Ethiopian Jews were leaving from Addis Ababa, also bound for Israel. Biruk had given Emama the name of the group leader and she contacted him as soon as she could. She made arrangements to join him using the money Ayat had left for her to take a bus to Dero-woha.

"When did you arrive?" Debritu asked, as she held her mother's hand tightly, afraid to let it go.

"My group traveled through Sudan quickly and we made it to Israel a week ago on one of the first planes to arrive," Emama said. It turned out that her trek through Ethiopia and Sudan to Jerusalem had been very much like the one that Debritu and her brothers had just completed. Emama went on to tell her children that when she arrived she had made a friend who spoke Amharic in the Jewish Agency, the organization that helped all new immigrants in Israel.

"My friend helped me get a job greeting new Ethiopian immigrants as they arrived at the airport," Emama said. This way, she could watch each plane unload, hoping that she could catch sight of her children.

In the meantime, Emama had been living near the airport with other people who had recently arrived from Ethiopia. For the past week, she had traveled back and forth daily with a group of workers from the government's immigration department. Although each plane brought relief that more Beyta Israel had survived the difficult journey to Israel, Emama could not relax until her children finally came off the plane.

"What about your health?" Debritu asked, holding her mother's hand. "Do you need doctors any more?"

"I am much better," Emama answered with a sigh, "Especially now that I have my family again. I don't think I'll need to see a doctor for a very long time."

The family huddled together as they described their journeys. Emama listened carefully while Debritu and Ferdu recounted their trip and how sick Asefa had gotten.

"He almost died," Debritu whispered. They cried together as they remembered the many Ethiopians who had perished along the way.

Finally, Ferdu asked his mother, "What is it like here in Israel?"

"It is a strange place here," Emama said. "Very different from Ethiopia."

"I think I know what you mean," Debritu said, thinking of her first impressions. Her mother was quiet.

For a minute, Debritu felt worried again. "How will we fit in here?" she asked her mother.

"Our new life begins now," Emama said with a sigh. "It will be a challenge, but at least we will be together."

"Where will we live?" Debritu asked.

"They will be taking us to an absorption center, which is a new housing project in Jerusalem, where we will live with others who have arrived from Ethiopia. There will be Hebrew classes and teachers to help us adjust to the different ways of life here," Emama said as she guided her children towards a bus.

Inside the bus, Debritu sat by a window and looked out at the cars, trucks and other buses along the wide highway. She had never seen such a busy road. As they made their way up the hills leading to Jerusalem and through the Latrun valley, she could see abandoned army trucks left as a reminder of the battles that had taken place there. When the bus turned the corner off the highway into the city, Debritu looked out at the limestone buildings that spread out, covering the hills around her. She stared at the Hebrew writing on the buildings and signs, wondering what everything meant. Jerusalem, with its mix of modern and ancient buildings and streets, wasn't anything like what she had imagined. Debritu sighed as she glanced over at Asefa, who was sitting in the seat next to her.

"Are we almost there yet?" Asefa asked, as he clutched his sister's skirt in his hand.

"Yes," Debritu answered with a smile. "We're almost home."

* * *

Chapter Eleven
THE EMERALD'S RETURN
March 1986

"Is this where King Solomon's Temple stood?" Debritu asked her guide.

Debritu had been in Jerusalem for over a year now. She had spent most of her time in the absorption center learning to speak the Hebrew language and getting used to the new food. This was the first time she had ventured out to see the sights of the city. She and her new friends had decided to take a guided tour through the tunnels and digs near the Western Wall, the only remnant of King Solomon's Temple. People were standing along the ancient stones, thinking about a different era.

"Yes," said the guide, as the group looked down into the tunnels where archaeologists had dug out ancient sites.

"Who will go down into those tunnels?" Debritu asked.

"No one," the guide said. "The tunnels are too close to an ancient cemetery. They are being closed forever."

Debritu looked down at the dig and waited for everyone to pass. Then she thought about the promise she had made to her grandmother back in Ethiopia.

"Read the note and do what it says," her grandmother had told her. And now that she had learned Hebrew, she could read the note.

"Return the emerald to where it belongs," the note said.

Slowly Debritu opened her hand and dropped the emerald, still wrapped in the cotton sleeve she had made for it, down into the tunnel.

Then she turned towards her group of friends and ran to catch up.

* * *

Epilogue

THOUGH SOME OF THE STORY HAS BEEN CHANGED, the character of Debritu is based on a real person. When she finally arrived in Israel, the real Debritu changed her name to Shula. Her mother and brothers also took new names. The real Biruk and Enanu arrived safely in Israel soon after Debritu. Her father survived, and he, her grandfather and grandmother eventually joined the family several years later.

The real Shula went to a boarding school in Tel Aviv, where she learned Hebrew, and then she attended high school. She studied at the Hebrew University of Jerusalem and has a Masters degree in education.

In the summer of 2004, Shula returned to Ethiopia for the first time since her departure 20 years before. Although the little village where Shula lived with her grandparents no longer existed, the town of Gedebye was still there. Almost all of the Jews in the area, however, were gone.

The story of Aleesha is, of course, a work of fiction, but it is based on the many stories that have come to us from Ethiopia and elsewhere. Wherever possible, attention has been paid to the details of the time. Deviations, however, do occur. For example, modern place names have been used instead of historical ones so that the reader will be better able to identify geographic references.

As for the original Ark of the Covenant, many legends claim ownership to its whereabouts. Some historians report that the Ark was demolished when the Babylonians invaded Jerusalem and destroyed the first Temple. Others say that the Ark remained in Elephantine, Egypt. Then there are those who believe that the Ark is hidden in a chapel just beside the Church of St. Mary of Zion in the ancient city of Axum, in the northern Ethiopian highlands. No one knows for sure, although Ethiopian Christian priests guard the chapel carefully and allow no visitors to enter. Every day, dozens of Ethiopians and other visitors flock to the dusty city of Axum and mill about outside the chapel, hoping to catch a glimpse of something inside. They feel the excitement of the ancient mystery that the Ark of the Covenant has come to represent.

* * *

Timeline

DAUGHTERS OF THE ARK

Date	Event
Date	**Event**
1446 B.C.E.	Moses gives the Ten Commandments to the Israelites. An Ark is later built to enclose it.
966 B.C.E.	King Solomon begins construction of the Temple in Jerusalem to house the Ark.
961 B.C.E.	The Queen of Sheba travels to Jerusalem from Axum to visit King Solomon and stays six months.
941 B.C.E.	The Queen of Sheba's son, Prince Menelik, travels to Jerusalem. He studies at the Temple in Jerusalem for two years.
939 B.C.E.	The eldest sons of King Solomon's priests and their families accompany Prince Menelik back to Ethiopia.

938 B.C.E.	Prince Menelik and his entourage reach Ethiopia after traveling for approximately one year.
586 B.C.E.	The Babylonian army lays siege to Jerusalem, the First Temple is destroyed, and the twelve tribes of Israel are exiled for the first time.
583 B.C.E.	The Israelites return to Jerusalem and work begins on the Second Temple.
70 C.E.	The Second Temple is destroyed and the Israelites are exiled from Jerusalem for the second time.
300 to 600	Christianity comes to Ethiopia and is eventually adopted by the Ethiopian empire.
700	Islam arrives in Ethiopia.
990	Yehudit, the warrior-queen believed to be a Beyta Israel, takes power in Ethiopia and rules for approximately forty years.
1270 to 1930	A succession of Christian Ethiopian monarchs rule over Ethiopia.

1930	Haile Selassie becomes Emperor. Formerly known as Ras Tafari, Haile Selassie (whose name means Hail the Trinity) is believed to be the 225th direct-line descendant of Prince Menelik.
1948	The modern State of Israel is established and brings in previously dispersed Jewish communities.
1974	Haile Selassie is overthrown by revolutionaries, beginning a 17-year military dictatorship in Ethiopia.
1982-1985	Ethiopia suffers from a recurring drought and famine. Almost one million people die.
1984	Operation Moses, a mass exodus of the Ethiopian Jews to Israel, is organized. Between 7,000 and 8,000 Beyta Israel, mostly from the Gondor area, are airlifted from Sudan to Jerusalem by the Israeli military.
1991	Operation Solomon – another 15,000 Beyta Israel are airlifted to Israel.

* * *

Glossary

Hebrew words

Abba – father in Hebrew

Habash – Ethiopia in ancient Hebrew

Ima – mother

Labreeyute – to your health

Shalom – hello

Amharic words

Abbat – father

Amharic – a language spoken in Ethiopia

Ayat – grandfather

Beyta Israel – Ethiopian Jews

Birr – Ethiopian currency

Budas – bad spirits

Emama – mother

Falasha – exiled, derogatory word for Ethiopian Jew

Farenje – white foreigner

Ge'ez – ancient Ethiopian language

Gojjo – hut

Imita – grandmother
Injara – Ethiopian round flat bread
Kess, Kessotch – priest, priests
Orit – the Bible
Sanbat – Sabbath
Shemma – shawl
Shiftas – bandits
Teff – type of grain
Tota – monkey

* * *

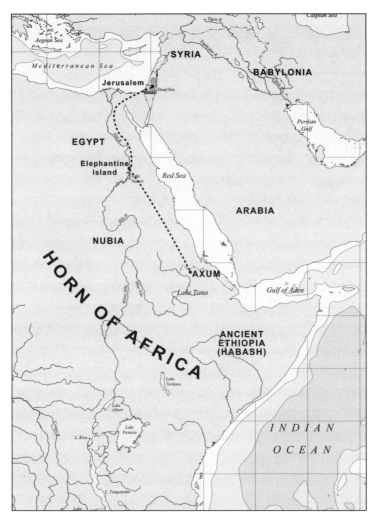

Aleesha's Journey
(Ancient Middle East and Northeast Africa)

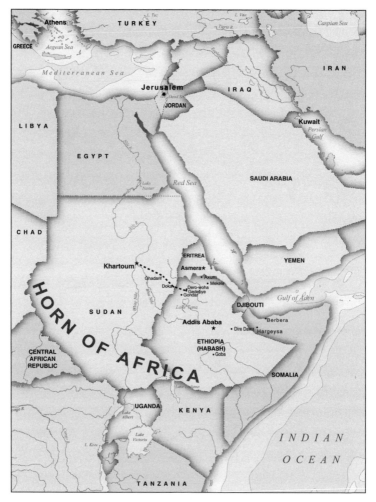

Debritu's Journey *(1984)*
*(From Khartoum, Debritu and her brothers flew to
Israel via France.)*

Debritu (Shula) grew up in homes like these in Ethiopia.

Children in the streets of Gedebye, a town near the village where Debritu lived.

A girl pounding garlic and preparing a meal in Gedebye.

The countryside near Gedebye.

A boy making sesame oil with the help of a camel.

A woman weaving.

Market day in Axum, Ethiopia.

Ethiopian children in Gondar.

Some people say that the Ark of the Covenant is kept in this building, the Church of St. Mary of Zion in Axum. Only one appointed priest is ever allowed inside.

Debritu (Shula) and her brothers traveled across
landscapes like these to reach Sudan.

Shula on her first trip back to Ethopia.

Shula (formerly Debritu) with her two children, Noam and Amit, in Israel today.

The author at the ruins of the Queen of Sheba's Palace
outside Axum.

Anna Morgan is a journalist who writes for newspapers
and magazines. She has traveled extensively and interviewed
people from all over the world, including one of the heroines
of this book. Anna lives in Toronto with her husband and
children. *Daughters of the Ark* is her first book.

Acknowledgments

I WOULD LIKE TO THANK Sarah Silberstein Swartz, Margie Wolfe, Laura McCurdy and the team at Second Story Press for their help and encouragement, Steven Kaplan for his comments, my colleagues at the Canadian Jewish News for their lively debates and, of course, Shula Mola for sharing her life story with me. I would also like to thank the Ontario Arts Council for its support. I am grateful to Galila Turkienicz, Mark, Rachael and Eli Turkienicz for their patience and continuous support. Most of all, I am indebted to Ed, Jennie, Jacob and Orly, for listening to and reading my drafts and re-drafts and reminding me that all stories do, eventually, come to an end.

* * *